GIVE NO GROUND

GIVE NO GROUND

P.I.V.O.T. LAB CHRONICLES™ BOOK FIVE

MICHAEL ANDERLE

LMBPN Publishing
PMB 196, 2540 South Maryland Pkwy
Las Vegas, NV 89109

First US Edition, December, 2020
(Previously published as a part of *Choosing What Matters*)
eBook ISBN: 978-1-64971-378-0
Print ISBN: 978-1-64971-379-7

CHAPTER ONE

The first thing Dotty was aware of was the smell. Her last recollection was of lying in a private room in Insea, her form that of a dwarf. She had been Dotty Hunt—or, as the dwarves called her, *Zauberer* Hunt—a woman who had protected magical artifacts made by the dwarves.

Now, as part of an ongoing experiment within the virtual-reality world of PIVOT, she was changing bodies. Partly for the sake of curiosity, she had chosen to be an orc. She had seen numerous humans, dwarves, and elves in the world of PIVOT thus far, but no orcs. From what she understood, they kept to themselves and the mystery intrigued her.

The other reason for her choice was vanity—in a very backward way, of course. As a young girl raised soon after the Great Depression and coming of age in the wake of World War II, she had known there were very specific expectations for a girl of her social class.

Especially an attractive girl.

She had spent hours each week worrying that she wasn't pretty enough or that what good looks she had would slip away.

So many times, she had gone to bed hungry to make sure she would still fit into her dresses and she had agonized as the years went by about every wrinkle and gray hair. When she had the chance to go into the video game world of PIVOT, she'd had one request. She wanted to be ugly.

Being a dwarf had given her the permission she needed to eat as much as she wanted, not worry in the slightest about her hair, and in general, live her life without the constant, draining need to focus on her appearance.

Although she wasn't sure she'd fully committed to the ugliness.

When she opened her eyes, her gaze settled on the branches of a tree above her. Its trunk split into a wide canopy of branches, almost like an umbrella, and its leaves were a beautiful, brilliant green. She sat, winced at the ache in her back—she'd no doubt been lying down too long—and surveyed the area around her.

There was…nothing at all.

"Prima?" She called to the virtual reality's resident AI. "Where the heck am I? And what do I smell?"

"You're in the Orcish Hinterlands," Prima replied. *"As for the smell…look down."*

"Did I step in something? Oh, God, was I *lying* in it?" Dotty twisted and tried to look at her back but failed, of course.

She stopped when she noticed her body. Her skin could still pass for what she considered to be flesh-toned, but the brown shade carried a distinct greenish undertone. She turned her hands to study them curiously. They were unnaturally large hands with callused palms and attached to thick, muscled forearms. She wiggled her toes and focused on them. Her feet were bare, although she didn't feel any discomfort. They must be as callused as her hands.

There was still the smell to deal with, however. She shook out the rough fabric of her tunic and examined her pants, which were made of the same fabric.

Finally, she realized the terrible truth.

"It's *me*," she said in horror. "The smell is *me*."

"Yes, that's what I was trying to tell you."

"Will I smell like this for the whole game?" She looked skyward—a reflex she had never quite shaken when it came to talking to Prima—and glared. "Are you…you didn't—you knew I wanted to be an orc and you never mentioned this?"

"Of course not." The AI sounded halfway between innocently confused and wickedly pleased. *"You said you wanted to be ugly. By human standards, orcs best fit that description. Smell was not a factor you wanted to consider."*

"You could have warned me!"

"Again, smell was not a factor you—"

"I didn't tell you that I preferred to wake up without a broken arm, but you worked that one out!" She waved her hands and the smell wafted to her nose again. "Oh, that is *rank*."

"I'm told one gets used to things like that. Your smell is not out of the usual parameters for orcs, at any rate."

"That's another thing," Dotty said. "Where are the other orcs?"

"Ah!" Now, Prima sounded excited. *"Your village was entirely wiped out by a plague. Except for you, of course."*

"Lovely." Not for the first time, she reflected that the AI didn't have the best grasp of human emotion—specifically, the difference between interesting and good.

"You are now searching for a new home to the west," she explained. *"You'll find it in the shadow of that mountain."*

She discerned the rough outline of the mountain nearby and sighed. "And of course, they won't pelt me with stones and make me leave, because…" She waved her hands for Prima to fill in the blank.

"You'll have to see, won't you?"

With another heavy sigh, she looked around. A plain wooden staff and something square, wrapped in tattered cloth, lay beside her. Curiously, she crouched and unwrapped it to find a very familiar book.

The last time she had seen it, of course, it had been inscribed with dwarven runes and it had been gifted to her dwarven avatar. Now, it was written in a gorgeous script that was unlike anything she had seen before. The golden clasp was inscribed with patterns that looked like an interlocking set of sticks spaced according to a geometric pattern.

It was still a book of earth magic, but the spells were now conceptualized according to orcish culture. She raised her eyebrows.

Then she realized how thirsty she was.

"I don't suppose I have any food."

"Nope."

"Delightful." She rewrapped the book and set off toward the mountain in the distance. "So what's my name now? I doubt Dotty works for an orc."

"Strangely, it does. It's spelled D-A-H-T-I in orcish, but it is an orcish name."

"Huh. Dahti." Dotty—or, she supposed, Dahti—pushed forward, very aware of the sun beating down on her. The mountain was at least an hour or two away by foot, and she honestly wasn't sure if the sun would have burned or sickened her by then. She scanned the horizon and altered her course slightly when she saw a small stand of trees. Hopefully, there would be shade and water there.

The smell aside, the new body moved well. She strode easily, struck the ground with her walking stick, and hummed quietly on occasion. It had been comfortable, in a certain way, to return to her own body, but there were things she hadn't missed—weakness, aching joints, and the ever-present pain in her stomach.

She had gone into the game world again before she found out whether the cancer in her abdomen had grown or not. Her choice to spend her last months in a virtual world instead of having chemotherapy had unsettled her children, but Dotty did not regret it in the least. In this world and the young avatars she was given, her heart pumped strongly and her muscles worked without tiring.

Still, despite her strength, she was tired when she reached the oasis. Her steps had become slower and her bare feet were sore and hot. She could feel her lips close to cracking from being parched, and she had the suspicious thought that the more she walked toward it, the farther away the mountain became.

"It's an optical illusion," Prima said when she accused her of that. She had the mental image of the AI rolling its eyes. *"There's no weird magic going on, and I am not messing with you."*

"That's reassuring." Her voice emerged with an ungraceful squeak. She cleared her throat and forced herself to take the last few steps into the shade of the trees. "Oh, thank goodness." She sank to her knees. The earth there was only marginally less hot, but she would take it. A spring—little more than a puddle if the truth be told—was only a few feet away. She rested for a moment before she crawled to it and scrambled back a moment later.

Laughter echoed inside her head.

Dahti glared at the sky, steeled herself, and crawled forward again to look at her reflection in the water.

She had only the faintest stubble on her head—a skim of her hand confirmed that the hair was short and faintly bristly like velvet—and small tusks at the corners of her mouth. How had she not noticed those? She poked her tongue at them. They were certainly there.

Her nose was strongly arched, her cheekbones high, and her mouth full but small. All of the features appeared to be subtly out of scale with one another. None of that was apparent from the first, however, because her face was half-covered by a geometric tattoo.

Her sigh was all she could manage. She had always insisted that her children not get any tattoos and had the feeling that Prima had particularly enjoyed making this part of the avatar.

"What? You said you wanted to be ugly. By human standards, the scale of your features counts as ugly. Also, the green. The tattoo is a matter of taste, of course."

"So you went above and beyond," Dahti muttered. She stooped and slurped water into her mouth. It was difficult to not drink deeply, but she remembered that too much water too quickly might make her throw up and she couldn't afford that.

Her thirst assuaged, she sat until the sun began to sink before she stood and continued toward the mountain. A short distance later, she noticed smoke rising against the backdrop of the mountain—a sharp, treeless rise in the middle of the plains with veins running down its flanks.

It took her a while to realize that she could see the village. The buildings were covered and thatched with grass, which made them blend well into the landscape around them. It was only the regular shape of the roofs that caught her eye.

Not long after, the sound of children playing carried to her. She smiled and pushed on through the grass. If children were allowed to run and play, this settlement must be both prosperous enough that they weren't working and safe enough that there weren't patrols.

That was as far as she got in her musings before one of them barreled into her at high speed.

"Whoa." She staggered sideways and managed to drop the book on her foot.

Clumsy, Level 8, the game told her.

Dahti rolled her eyes and looked for the child. He had fallen and turned to look at her now with wide gray eyes. His skin was a dusky red, his frame short and compact. Before she could explain her presence, he scrambled to his feet and ran away, shrieking that there was a stranger in the grass.

She decided she had better go and explain herself. With a sigh, she picked the book up and followed the sound of his yells into the village.

Hopefully, these orcs didn't have a "shoot first and ask questions later" policy.

CHAPTER TWO

It was relatively easy to tell when the child attracted attention because the sound of chatter in the village ceased. Dahti waited, pushed aside the grass in the path the child had left, and sighed when she heard the shouts begin.

Thankfully, she reached the open square before the warriors with weapons approached. They skidded to a stop—ranging from men and women with spears to a farmer with a scythe and a cook with a bloodstained cleaver—and she dropped her book and staff hastily and put her hands up.

"I am Dahti," she said clearly. "I mean none of you harm. I am seeking shelter after my village was destroyed."

They looked at one another and moved their weapons aside.

None of them dropped the weapons, she noted, but no one seemed ready to attack at present. She'd take it.

"Who destroyed your village?" asked an older man.

"A sickness." She waited for them to drive her away. "I am the only survivor."

To her surprise, they didn't seem upset at all. They exchanged looks before people moved closer...closer...closer... She took a step back but they simply pushed forward. Their hands touched her hair, her shoulders, her arms, and her face.

She held utterly still and hoped no one was about to stab her. For all she knew, these people had no idea how germs were transmitted, but surely *everyone* knew to steer clear of those who had a disease.

It all became moot when the crowd parted and a grumpy older man with white scraggly hair, his back slightly hunched, trudged ponderously toward her. He extended his staff to tilt her chin up and her head side to side. After a moment, he seized one hand and turned it in his, then pulled her head down to stare into her eyes. When he released her, she fought the urge to flee into the underbrush.

He nodded at those assembled. "She speaks true. She is a carrier of Strength."

"Um…" A little bewildered, she looked around at those who had closed around her once more and now patted her skin with their hands. "I beg your pardon?"

The orc turned to her. His head was cocked curiously. "Did you have no shaman in your village? Or were your ways so different from ours, then?"

Dahti stumbled over her words as she tried to come up with a not-quite-lie. "I, ah—he mentioned something when the illness came, but he was taken quickly—"

"It had been a long time, then, since your tribe dealt with illness." He nodded. "Those who survive such events are bearers of great strength. When they journey forth, they bring that strength to their next home. You have granted us your strength so we will grant you wisdom in return. This is why we welcome you gladly. We will expect great things from your line."

"From my—wait a minute." She hurried after him. "I have no intention to bear children."

He only chuckled.

"I mean it." She took a gamble. "I…also planned to study as a shaman. I might have been taken as an apprentice if ours had not died."

At that, he stopped and gave her an intrigued look. "You? You would be a shaman? Hmmm." He considered this as he paced slowly and muttered quietly as if in discussion with himself. She made out a few scattered phrases—"most unusual," "a great boon to the order," "dare I break tradition?"

She waited.

At long last, he turned to her and narrowed his eyes. "You are healthy, yes. You have strength, yes. But to fight the gods, you must have more than strength of body. You require strength of mind, and this is what I shall test. Come with me."

Dahti looked curiously at the now silent group around her before she turned to follow the shaman and only caught the faintest glimmer from the corner of her eye when he gestured.

It was a subtle gesture but every sense went on high alert. She had to force herself to take another step rather than freeze, then another, her demeanor calm.

A battle cry split the air behind her.

Out of instinct, she turned. She had been trained in combat by a dwarf who had cheerful irreverence for everyone and every-thing and who favored the element of surprise in all things. It was for him, therefore, that she yelled, "Stooooooout!" as she thumped the heavy book across her attacker's face.

The man, armed with a staff he'd raised over his head, went down like a pile of bricks.

Thoroughly bewildered, she stared at him, then turned at a strange choking noise from behind her. To her surprise, the shaman was laughing.

"Heh." He nodded at her. "Not bad, young one, not bad. Now, come this way and we'll find you a hut."

Again, she followed and expected to be assaulted more than anything else, but everyone seemed to have taken the attack—and her retaliation—in stride. A few orcs hauled their fallen companion away, dragging him none too gently by the limbs while a few of the kids began to recreate the battle with gales of laughter.

Dahti shook her head, baffled, and hurried after the old orc.

"Can I ask something?" she asked him.

He looked at her in a way that brought to mind the response she'd given her children many a time—"it sounds like you just did."

She swallowed. "Why did you trust me? I didn't expect such a welcome." It couldn't merely be, surely, that she was the protagonist of the game. She realized with a jolt that she would be disappointed if that were the case.

"Your village was very different," the shaman guessed. "Earth tribes can be like that."

Dahti looked at his red-tinted skin. They must have drawn conclusions from her appearance that she was not knowledgeable enough to understand.

"The shaman who trained me used to say fire tribes were the most open," the shaman said contemplatively, "that we gobble up anything that will strengthen us like a hungry flame. Wind, now, they keep to themselves, and the water…" He shook his head. "We are less for their loss. The earth tribes, though, they will accept anyone but only after a time, as slowly as one tree grows around another."

His words made her think back on her life. It was an apt description of many of her family members, enough so that she smiled. "I've met many of all inclinations."

"Ah, but you speak of people, not tribes." He bonked her on the head with his staff, hard enough that she stood back with a dazed shake of her head. "Come along, Earth Apprentice."

They had no sooner resumed walking when a loud boom echoed and she ducked reflexively. Everyone was looking in one direction—up.

With her heart in her throat, she followed the direction of

their focus and froze. A plume of white smoke now billowed out of the top of the mountain. Her jaw dropped.

"This is…a *volcano*?" How had she missed the shape of it? Unless it had never erupted before. She caught the shaman's arm. "We have to go. Right now."

He looked at her, wary and watchful. "Volcano? I did not know earth tribes had a name for them."

"That's not the important part!" She waved her hands. "Please. *Please*, come, we have to go."

"We must face our god," he told her slowly. "In all things, there is balance. In all relationships, there must be a give and take. We live off the land, we accept its blessings, and in return, we must face the hunger of its gods."

Her heart was doing a strange double-time beat in her chest. "There is no way to face this god and survive."

"Perhaps not." He looked suddenly wary. "Perhaps, though, that is why your tribe was taken, Earth Apprentice—they refused to honor their obligations. When the gods creep out of their lairs and their wings block out the sun, those they choose must face their fate."

Dahti stared at him, open-mouthed. She was so horrified, she didn't know how to reply.

Harold would have laughed himself sick if he heard she'd been rendered speechless by anything. She massaged her temples and tried to think of something—anything—to say.

What came out of her mouth was, "Wings?"

She was glad her subconscious had caught that fact because the rest of her had been fixated on fiery death.

The shaman tilted his head to the side again. "Yes. The gods awaken and they come to feast upon the world. The legends always describe wings."

"Ohhhh." She was getting a headache. "So, *you* think the top of that mountain is smoking because there's a god inside—with wings—who'll come out and eat…maybe us or maybe only some other stuff?"

He looked at her as if she were insane. "Yes. Precisely."

His entire demeanor was so calm and matter of fact that she wanted to sob in frustration. "This mountain. Is. A volcano. There is no god and there are no wings, only rock that is hot beyond anything you can imagine. The top of the mountain will blow off and the rock and ash will rain on this village. Everyone here *will* die, and there will be nothing gained for *anyone*."

"This is, indeed," he said gravely, "why your village was struck down. Yet you must see, child, that they ignored the laws of nature—and that you were spared for a reason. You serve as an omen. You were given the chance for redemption."

"Bullshit," Dahti said before she could stop herself. "If I was spared for a greater purpose, it was helping all of you avoid a needless death. There are children in this village—those who look to you for guidance—and you cannot honestly tell me you think the gods require their sacrifice!"

"It is the way of the world." The shaman raised his shoulders. "Child, you want to argue, I see that. Come. Learn. In time, as the seasons pass and the moon waxes and wanes, your wisdom will grow and you will see the fullness of the seasons—hunger and feast, curse and blessing. All things ebb and flow in this world."

He left her staring after him.

"Prima?" she whispered. "What do I do?"

"What do you want to do?"

"I want to run," she said at once. "But if I go, the children will have no chance to leave. But can I convince any of them, do you think, even if I stay?"

"It is up to you to try or not—not knowing the outcome, only choosing as best you can."

"I hope *you* someday wind up in a game with someone who gives you cryptic advice all the time," she muttered.

"*I am,*" the AI said, amused. "*I don't understand half the things you people do.*"

Dahti was startled into a laugh. She looked at the village and the people who still snuck glances at her, then turned to the shaman who waited for her at the door of an empty hut.

"I can't let them die because it was too difficult to explain volcanos," she said finally.

"*Mmm, interesting.*"

By now, she'd had enough dealings with the AI to know better than to ask for details of what that meant. She rolled her eyes and hurried to her new house. It was time to come up with new, pseudo-religious stories to convince the tribe of the need to leave.

CHAPTER THREE

With a new member of the village and the imminent arrival of a god, a feast ensued that included singing, dancing, and helping upon helping of a stew that was so spicy, it made Dahti's eyes water. The villagers all laughed uproariously at her for gulping water and fruit juice, but they openly approved of her managing to finish her plate.

It was sheer discipline that enabled her to do so. She had been raised after the depression, after all. One never refused food, even if it made one want to drink the entirety of the great lakes and possibly cut one's tongue off.

Boy, would her family be surprised if she came back from this round of the game enjoying curries. She wondered if that might be sooner rather than later if the volcano exploded unexpectedly.

Whether it was the spice, the dancing, or simply the joy of being in a non-aching body again, she sang and danced enthusiastically with the villagers, late into the night. When she finally retired to her little hut, it was with her head unclouded by alcohol but her feet sore and her muscles tingling with exhaustion.

She woke to sunlight slanting in the door—undoubtedly the

reason why all the huts faced east—and groaned when she pushed up. Every muscle ached after the last day's exertions, although she was thankfully not sunburned.

Breakfast was more of the same spicy curry, along with introductions to so many people that she soon lost count. In her head, she categorized people the same way she had in the dwarven caravan, giving them nicknames according to their physical characteristics. One was Copper Necklace, another Smiles-a-lot, and a third was Jumper—a young girl who liked to climb anything she could and leap off.

Dahti was fairly sure the girl's mother must already have completely white hair.

She had learned a few things in her eighty-four years, and one of them was that if you wanted someone to listen to you, you had to do a fair amount of listening yourself first. Accordingly, she spent much of her morning wandering to various fires and doors, learning people's names again, and listening to them speak fondly of their spouses and children.

A few mothers slyly suggested that they had fine, strong sons, a suggestion she relentlessly pretended to not understand until she could escape the conversation. The shaman hadn't been lying when he said great things were expected of a Strength-bearer's lineage—it was only a matter of time, she suspected, until dowries were brought into the mix.

Although sore, she was still able to play a few rounds of a hopping game with the children of the village, along with something that seemed roughly comparable to tag. By lunch, when she sank into the shadows of her hut to pant, she was fairly sure she could find common ground with these villagers. They weren't so different from people anywhere else, after all.

Were they?

The shaman arrived in the doorway with a bowl of food, and when she peeked inside, she saw plain rice. Her face must have lit up because he laughed.

"After a few meals of our food, I thought you deserved something more to your tastes."

Dahti hastily swallowed a mouthful of rice. "I'm sure I'll get used to the spice."

"In time, I'm sure." He stood patiently until she realized he was waiting for an invitation and gestured to the floor on the other side of the firepit. He sat as well. "So. Perhaps you are rethinking your belief that we are misguided? You have met the people and listened to their stories."

Carefully, she considered her words as she savored the last mouthful of rice.

"I am not as young as I look," she said finally. "I cannot explain it, shaman, but I am not a youthful risk-taker. I believe in caution, and I have seen something of the world. The people I have seen— be they human, dwarf, or orc—are more alike than they are different."

"What of the elves?" He cocked an eyebrow.

"I haven't had a chance to speak to any elves," she said somewhat bitterly. "They always introduced themselves blade-first."

He considered her with quiet interest. "You've fought elves? Interesting. Your village must have been very different if you mixed with so many people. Perhaps that is why you disregard our people's ways."

"Perhaps," she said and sighed. "Sir…ah, what does one call a shaman?"

"So formal. There's no need for that."

Dahti shrugged. "Well, then. When I said I've seen many people, it was true. I've seen those who believed in no gods at all, some who believed in many, some who believed in only one, and others who believed in one with many faces. All had beliefs that held them back and even endangered them. But none were stupid. They had those beliefs for a reason."

"You think," the shaman said slowly, "that we have a reason for our beliefs but that our beliefs are not true?"

His response surprised her and she stared at him for a moment. It wasn't a delicate way of putting it, but at eighty-four, she was beyond delicacy. "Yes," she said finally. "I've been in places, sir, where simply the difference between our skin colors would be enough for terrible violence—and all who are here would say that was a senseless belief, yes? As we shed that, perhaps you will shed this."

He shook his head. "It is a dangerous thing to change the order of the world, young one—or however young you may be."

"A common logical fallacy," she said. Her grandson James would be laughing his head off right about now, as he was the one who'd taught her that phrase when he considered becoming a philosophy major. In that conversation, of course, *he* had been the one arguing for change. "One perceives making a change as the only active choice. Why risk change? Because choosing to stay the same is also a choice and it is also risky."

The shaman settled back to look at her. "The gods provide. They give us rains and they give us the beasts that roam the land. Should we refuse their bargain, our descendants—or those of our fellow tribes—will be afflicted." He hesitated. "As yours were. To try to avoid death is to cheat the gods, and they do not like being cheated."

She looked out at the people in the village. They glanced frequently at the mountain but did not seem fearful. "They don't know what the god's return means, do they?"

"They do." He smiled. "All orcs die in time, some as they hunt and others from sickness. Still, few rush to meet it. Some will hope they are passed over and yet others will pray that their children are not chosen."

Dahti tried to keep her voice level but it trembled. "Shaman, to die in fire and ash—it is a terrible, terrible death."

His expression flickered and he bowed his head. "Many deaths are terrible. In the halls of our ancestors, though, we will walk without pain."

An idea formed in her head. She would have no lineage in the game, and thus had an advantage. "Tell me this—are the gods just?"

He gave her a surprised look. "How do you mean?"

"Do they give people only what they deserve?" she asked. "You say my tribe paid for the sins of its ancestors. That is not just. Could another pay for…my sins?"

"It is difficult to know," he said thoughtfully. "I am curious as to why you ask."

Now she was in a bind because she couldn't tell him. If she were to subvert the plan and somehow spirit these people away, they might spend the rest of their lives fearing reprisal. She did not want to frighten them with that.

On the other hand, if they knew that she, and she alone, would be blamed, she could easily shoulder the guilt of whatever lies and stories she made up to get them away from this volcano. She needed time to think. For one thing, she did not even know how she could lie well enough to lure people away, not when their shaman told them to sacrifice themselves.

"It seems lopsided," she said finally. "The gods give and then they take, and humanity—orcs, I mean—are offered no choice in the matter."

The shaman looked down and said quietly, "I once thought as you do."

Something in his voice caught her attention, and Dahti looked closely at him. "You *once* did…or you *still* do?"

He gave her a wry look. "I do not like the bargain," he said frankly, "but I have seen visions and heard stories. The gods exist all over this land. There is no running from them. There is no facing them, either, for they are creatures well beyond the skill of any warrior or shaman. After what happened to the water tribes—"

"What *did* happen to them?"

"You don't know?" He looked genuinely confused now. "They

were lost two generations ago. They were the most powerful of us and the most devout—and their gods turned on them."

She bolted to her feet, her fists clenched. "They did nothing wrong, and *still* they were killed? *Still* they were wiped out?"

"What would you have me do, young one?" He looked wearily at her. "Your people defied the gods and were punished for it. The water tribes did not and still, they were taken. Is it unjust? Yes. Do I wish I could stand against the gods? Yes, I wish it very much. But I cannot stand against them any more than I can stop the sun from rising. So I counsel my people to follow their faith, to hope to avoid the gods' notice, and to live as best they can, when they can. The gods are like famine or drought. They are beyond us. I will not stir my people to rebellion if it will only cause pain."

Dahti stared at him. She was still breathing hard, but her anger had begun to unravel. How often had she counseled her daughters on how to behave, even while they shouted at her that it wasn't fair that they had to hold their tongue, or put makeup on, or endure the harassment they got every day, simply for existing? How often had she counseled her sons on how to behave, even when they asked why *they* couldn't stay home with the children, why *they* weren't allowed to ask for help or admit weakness or show emotion?

Everyone has beliefs that hold them back, but they don't have them senselessly. She had only been trying to spare her children the pain that would come from others' disapproval. This shaman, too, was trying to spare his people.

She took a deep breath. "If I could…if I could stand against the god… If you could train me and take the villagers away, would you do it? Leave me behind to fight the god in your stead?" When he said nothing, she pressed on. "You know the gods have no interest in justice. The water tribes' death shows that. Let me at least *try* to free you from this one."

In the intensity of the discussion, she had barely noticed the rumbling, but it now made tiny rocks dance across the floor.

The shaman's shoulders slumped. "I would have done so, child, if there was time. But there is not." He looked at the village square, where people suddenly screamed and pointed. "The god is here."

He was resigned to death and had accepted it.

Dahti had not. She hauled him to his feet a moment later. "Start thinking of how to get them out of here," she told him. "Because the only hope now is to run. Get them moving. *Now*."

CHAPTER FOUR

With the plains stretching all around, she had no idea how she could possibly get the villagers moving quickly enough to outrun the volcano. She knew, on some distant level, that it was impossible to go quickly enough on foot, but she refused to listen to that certainty.

Even a slim chance of success was better than none, after all.

Briefly, Dahti entertained the thought of trying to stop the eruption with magic, but she finally shook her head at her foolishness. A few weeks before, she had almost drained her entire life force trying to trap a dozen wolves. The entire, explosive power of a volcano was unquestionably beyond her.

Her only option was to get all the villagers moving as quickly as possible. She took a single breath to compose herself—the air was already hot—and ducked out of the hut. The villagers were pointing at the mountain and she did not dare to look.

She couldn't lose her courage.

The child she called Jumper was crying, and she took her hand firmly and led her to where the shaman was speaking.

"We have been called into the plains," he shouted over the ever-present rumbling. "All must come now. Those who cannot walk quickly will be carried. Make sure all the members of your household are here and follow me!"

As they began their evacuation, she remained behind, steadfastly ignored the temptation to look at the mountain, and made a quick check through each building. She was careful to lift sleeping mats and open cupboards, aware that children might hide in the smallest spaces when they were frightened. She found only one old woman trying to dig up a stash of coins and hurried her out to where the village was walking away. Whether it was from shock or because she was the shaman's new de facto apprentice, the woman thankfully did not argue.

Then, with her book on her back and her staff in her hand, she hurried after the group. It did not take her long to catch up. The tribe moved as quickly as they could, but there was a limit to how fast their feet could take them and that wasn't as fast as ash and rock could rain down.

With her heart in her throat, she finally turned to look at the mountain.

It gave her some hope. The worst of the eruption had not happened yet. Black smoke billowed from the top—which *still* did not look like a volcano to her, although it must be—and she thought she could see a faint glow. As yet, there was no sign of lava flowing down the mountainsides or ash kicked into the air.

Maybe they had time. Dahti increased her pace and hurried through the group, offering encouraging smiles and nods to the villagers she recognized until she caught up with the shaman.

"Do we have a destination?" she asked in an undertone. "Or are we simply getting as far away as we can?"

He gave her a tense look. "I'm…well, I'm breaking all the traditions at once." He seemed to be bleakly amused by the fact.

"Yes?" She wanted to be amused but it was difficult when there was imminent death at her back. "And?"

"I'm taking them to the Cave of Trials," he told her with a sigh. "Only the shamans are ever supposed to go there. It is a holy place, and those who see it without—" He broke off at the look on her face.

She wasn't particularly interested in legends right now.

"There is water," he said finally, "and good earth for crops, and the warren of caves faces away from the mountain."

Her shoulders slumped with relief. "Thank God. Er…the gods." No, that wasn't right, either. "Um…do you have any gods aside from the ones who eat you?"

He looked quizzically at her. "When we get done with this particular adventure, you will tell me exactly what your tribe believed."

"I don't think you'll like it," Dahti muttered.

"At this point, I would be shocked if I did." He seemed amused by this too. "How you persuaded me to disobey all of my traditions is beyond me."

"No it's not," she replied smartly. "You know precisely why you did it. You've known your whole life that this system was wrong, and now that you have to choose between offering up the people you love to a certain and painful death or disobeying, you realize that you don't have it in you." She saw the self-hatred in his face and hastened to reassure him. "I don't think less of you for that, you know. Quite the opposite."

"I dishonor the sacrifices of those who went before," he said quietly.

She walked in silence for a few moments, pushed grass out of her way, and tried not to notice the way the sky grew dark around the mountain.

"They did the best they could," she said finally. "And you're doing the best you can. And—"

Behind them, a hollow boom issued and orcs screamed. She looked back at the billowing black smoke riddled with lightning.

They didn't have much time.

"How far are we?" she asked.

The shaman's reddish face had gone pale. "Two hours' walk, maybe more."

"Tell them to walk faster." Dahti very much doubted they had two hours to work with.

As it turned out, they did not. The next hour or more passed with children beginning to cry in hunger and thirst while the sky grew ever blacker and the beginning wisps of ash drifted on the wind. She could smell smoke, although it was less the comforting crackle of pine and more the charred, earthen scent of heated rock.

Then she thought about what it would mean if she smelled burning brush and realized there was a non-zero chance of the plains going up in flames around them.

She increased her pace.

The caves were in sight before she realized what they were. The ground sloped gently upward and the shaman pointed after a time to call that the caves were on the far side. She nodded and began to relay the message through the group when the top of the mountain split.

A burst of light erupted together with a thunderclap so loud she thought her eardrums had burst. Dahti fell, her ears ringing, aware that the ground seemed to move like the deck of a ship beneath her feet. Whether it was only her balance leaving her or the ground truly moving, she did not know.

She did not hear the screams because she could not hear anything. When she pushed to her feet, however, the orcs had stopped in their tracks, horror on their faces. Parents clutched children close and the elders of the group stared as if they had never expected to see such a thing.

Her heart in her throat, she turned to look.

The god was there and it was winged. Even so far away, she could see that immediately. Massive wings stretched wide and fanned the flames lazily as it arched its back. It was wreathed in smoke and it *was* the smoke while it bathed in the flames and created them.

"A dragon," she whispered. She couldn't hear her voice or anything beyond the beat of her blood. She thought she would pass out or maybe start laughing hysterically. "It's a *dragon.*"

Aghast, she whirled and caught someone's hand—Copper Necklace, whose face was horrified. Dahti shouted and since she couldn't hear herself, she could hope that what she said made sense. She waved frantically and urged them toward the caverns.

Toward whatever safety there might be.

Her feet pounded on the ground and a hasty glance showed that Copper Necklace was still holding her hand and the tribe now ran with her. Some of the children were still holding their ears and crying, but their parents clutched them and sprinted with single-minded determination.

When it came down to it, no one wanted to be sacrificed to a god. She pushed herself to move faster and prayed to every god she had ever heard of—but none of the dragons—that she could get the villagers through this.

"Prima!" she roared. "You'd better have a good plan!"

"I'd say you'd better have a good plan."

"Listen, you hunk of metal. If you let these people die, I will personally track you down and…and—" She was running out of breath.

"And?" Prima sounded intrigued.

"I'll think of something!" Dahti was aware that people were staring at her and she clamped her mouth shut on further threats.

A scream—she could hear things again—raised above the hubbub and she already knew what she would see when she looked over her shoulder.

She did anyway, whether to confirm her suspicions or torture herself, she wasn't quite sure. The dragon had taken flight and banked around the plume of smoke in lazy circles. It was still waking up—or perhaps it was drawing strength from the flames and the rock.

No wonder that mountain hadn't looked like a volcano.

In all honesty, she didn't care what it was doing as long as it didn't fly toward them. She ran with the villagers until a strange sound caught her attention.

Dahti knew what it sounded like, but it couldn't be that. After all, there were no boats nearby with sails fluttering in the wind. There was no canvas to pull taut in a gust.

Wings.

She twisted to look over her shoulder and swore. The dragon had seen them or smelled them, or maybe it merely flew in a random direction. It didn't matter, though, because it now headed directly toward them and closed the distance too quickly for the group to reach the caves.

"Run!" she screamed, and people put everything they had into their desperate flight.

The great beast's laughter sounded like thunder and rolling earth but there was no mistaking it for anything but laughter.

It liked the hunt.

White light stabbed across her eyes and she whipped her head around. The people around her slowed as well, and even the dragon's black-and-red head swung to look. She squinted to see the light shining from…a crystal?

Whatever it was, it was held aloft in the hand of someone who was cloaked and walked slowly through the grass, watching the dragon.

Someone *human*.

"Run," Dahti told the villagers. "Hide in the caves. I'll buy you time."

She sprinted toward the human with the crystal. They might not be friendly, but between a human and a vengeful dragon god, she didn't have any questions as to where she'd take her chances.

CHAPTER FIVE

It was only halfway to the stranger that Dahti remembered she could drop the book of spells. She assumed she wouldn't learn anything incredibly useful on short notice. Either she could pick it up later or she'd be fried to a crisp and it wouldn't matter.

Delightful.

The human had begun to run as well, and as soon as she was close enough to the figure to shout, she gave up entirely on any semblance of politeness.

"Tell me you're here to help!" she called.

"I am!" a woman called in response. She pushed the hood of her cloak back to reveal a pale, shockingly pretty face and dark hair. When she shrugged the cloak off entirely, Dahti saw that she wore black leather armor and carried two long daggers. "Justin sent me."

"Justin! Oh, thank God." She would have stopped and sagged with relief had she not been blown sideways when air buffeted her.

Dahti scrambled to her feet and turned, only for her jaw to drop open and for her to make what she was fairly sure was a very undignified sound of fear. She had already been terrified when she first saw the dragon. It was massive, after all, and there was no ambiguity in the long talons and sharp, gleaming teeth.

Up close, it was ten times more terrifying than her worst nightmare.

When it landed with a heavy thud, both women were upended. The earth shook with each step of its heavy feet and its breath seared the air. Dahti scrambled up in time to see its head come level with her.

She was surprised she didn't pass out with fear. Its snout was almost as tall as she was. Each slit-pupiled eye was shades of red and orange, and the front talons were as deep a black as onyx. In the space between the black scales, red glimmered like molten lava.

"Who are you?" it asked her. Its voice blew her back off her feet again and reverberated in her bones. "Both of you. An earth orc and a human. Two of you, who have taken my prey from me. Answer!"

Her irritation lent her courage and she stood slowly and glared at the beast. She was tired of being knocked down and she wasn't prepared to act contrite.

"I'm Dahti," she said simply. "And no one here is your prey."

"Oh, is that right?" It reared and began to circle them. "What of you, human? Who are you?"

"I am Zaara," the woman said. "I am apprentice to Mary, who commands the powers of death. I am friend to Justin, the savior of Insea."

"Insea!" The dragon gave a shout that might have been either derision or anger and launched flames skyward from its jaws before it snapped its teeth and whipped its head around to look at the woman again. "And what brings you to fire orc territory, *human*?"

"Why ask my name if you won't use it?" Zaara snapped.

Dahti decided she liked her.

"I asked who you were," the dragon said testily. "I don't care what you call yourself. Would you care about the names of insects?"

The woman folded her arms and glared.

Dahti stepped forward now. "Leave this place," she said clearly. "You have fooled these people into believing that you bring the rains and the beasts, but I will show them the truth no matter how many lifetimes it takes. I am privy to magics you have never seen before. I have powers you could not dream of. These people will no longer be your thralls."

The beast laughed. "Ah, do you think so? You may turn their heads for a time. But when I sweep from the skies and feast on their brethren, they will remember why they worshipped me. The next time a drought comes, they will tell themselves it is my wrath. I am their god and they are mine to devour." Its tongue flicked out.

"No more." She was practically vibrating with rage. "No more lies and no more deception. You are no god."

"What is a god?" It seemed amused now. "Something that is worshiped, something that is beyond them. I am both those things, little orc. Did you tell them you could save them from me?"

I told them you were a volcano without wings, Dahti wanted to say. She did not. Her miscalculation didn't need to be spread around at this juncture.

"You can't." The dragon brought its snout closer and feinted toward her so she danced back. It hissed a laugh at her. "When I devour you, they will understand who their god is and who is a false prophet. I shall keep my feasts, little meddler, and you—"

The crystal blazed to life once more and the dragon drew back with a hiss. Dahti covered her eyes with a cry of pain. The light was like the brightest sunlight, distilled and magnified into a beam. The sound of cracking stone was followed by a pained shriek.

"You're not invulnerable." Zaara's voice rolled through the air like thunder. "You're no more than any other creature, dragon. Begone!" The light flared once more and the creature shrieked again. A moment later, Zaara was at Dahti's side and shook her. "I think I bought us a moment," the woman whispered. "I—" She broke off and her nose wrinkled as she took in Dahti's smell.

"I *know*," she said, annoyed. "I smell to high heaven. I should have stayed a dwarf."

"Stayed a—" Zaara broke off and gaped at her before she shook her head. "No time. Explain later…if we survive."

She looked up to where the dragon had pushed off the earth and now circled while its wings beat strongly. A line across its side was grey-and-black, the molten look of it cooled, and it seemed to favor that wing.

"This is a being of fire and heat," Zaara said urgently, "so it's vulnerable to water, to cold, and to the absence of air. Can you summon any of those things? Justin said you were a wizard."

Dahti felt a surge of dread. "Justin may have overstated the case somewhat."

"Yeah, well, Justin took to it all fairly quickly, too." The woman's gaze tracked the dragon as it descended. "Also, we'll either kill it or it'll kill us—and I know which I'd prefer. Let's, uh…distract it and trade off. Take a potshot when it's advancing on me, and I'll do the same for you!"

She didn't wait for an answer and merely raced away in the grass with her blades flashing.

"Okay," Dahti said. "It looks like we're doing that, then." She stumbled as the dragon landed again and decided there was no time like the present for doing stupid things. "Hey, you stupid bugger! Over here! I bet your mother was a garden snake!"

"*As insults go, perhaps not your best work,*" Prima said after a moment. She sounded like she was trying not to laugh.

"Unfortunately, it probably is," she confessed. "I was never good at them."

"*Try harder,*" the AI advised her. "*You know what the dragon wants and what makes it mad. Maybe use those as themes? It's only a thought."*

She rolled her eyes. The beast swung its head from Dahti to Zaara as if trying to decide which to attack.

"The earth orcs joke about you!" Dahti called to the dragon. "Our gods are mighty and eternal. You're so weak you can't handle a little light thrown by a *human!*"

The dragon's head whipped around and it advanced on her. Its tail was lashing.

"Oh, good," she muttered. "It's working." To her adversary, she added, "This is your entire life? You sleep in a mountain in the middle of nowhere and come out every few hundred years to snack on prey that can't run away from you? And you expect me to think you're impressive? You expect people to *worship* you?"

It bared its teeth, snarled, and opened its jaws to inhale, and Dahti saw her chance. She thrust her hands out with the remembered smell in mind and conjured a cloud of thick dust for the dragon to suck down its throat instead of air.

Fire needed air, after all.

The creature choked and coughed with enough force to strip a nearby bush of all its leaves. It threw its head back and snarled in anger, but a flash of silver and blue caught her eye.

Zaara leapt out of the grass with speed and grace. Both daggers were drawn as she climbed nimbly up the dragon's side. She was laughably small compared to it, but she didn't look daunted even in the slightest. Power shone pale blue around her daggers—the same blue as the glitter of icebergs. As Dahti began to run, hoping to get out of the way of the dragon's retaliatory fireball, the woman planted her feet and plunged her daggers into the gaps between two of the black scales.

Whatever protective magic the dragon had, it was enough to hurl her off its back. She fell limply in the grass and was lost from view as the beast's tail lashed and it screamed in pain.

"Foolish," it snarled. It swung its head until its eyes fixed on

Dahti, and it began to advance. "Do you think to use winter against me? Winter is a weak thing. Frost is nothing compared to the power of a mountain's heart."

She stumbled back and tried desperately to turn the ground under her enemy's feet to shifting sand. It wouldn't do much except consume her mana bar, but she had no other ideas of how to distract it. She didn't have a frost enchantment on her knives, nor did she have any water magic.

The water orcs could have defeated this dragon, she thought resentfully. That was what was *supposed* to have happened in this world—the tribes were meant to band together, each tribe lending its shamans to defeat the other dragons.

When this particular dragon roared again, she decided her revelations could wait.

Whether Zaara was hurt or not, she didn't know. She surged into a sprint and raced toward the place where she'd seen the human woman fall. When she paused in a crushed avenue of grass, devoid of any bodies, she sighed with relief.

The dragon reared again and Dahti knew how quickly it could swing its head. She ran toward its feet instead and managed to avoid the surge of fire that set the grass ablaze.

Idiot, she cursed the beast. A wildfire here would do nothing except blight the land.

And make its predictions of famine come true. It was manufacturing adverse events for its benefit. Too lazy even to hunt its prey, it tried to make them believe they should trot gladly up the sides of the mountain and throw themselves into its mouth.

She didn't have much hope that she could do real damage, but she yanked her staff out and whacked the monster on the knee as she went past. Her weapon bounced off without seeming to do the slightest damage and her heart sank. She didn't have what it would take to defeat this, did she?

A yell and a flash of black told her that Zaara had launched another assault. The human streaked past her and stabbed at the beast's exposed belly, and Dahti followed up by whacking the open wound as hard as she could.

This time, the dragon noticed her. Its belly arched away and it lifted off with a speed that threw them down. As it circled, Zaara grasped Dahti's staff. She wrapped her hands around it and began to mutter urgently. Between her fingertips, frost crackled and spread.

"It's not my best work, but it'll have to do—come on!" She hauled her up. "Next time, we go at the same time. Strike the shoulder joints as hard as you can. I don't care what kind of magic you have, just *use* it!"

She nodded and the two women scrambled away from each other. The dragon had climbed into the sky and it now rocketed down with its eyes narrowed and flames streaking from its snout.

"Where are you, false prophet?" Its words boomed and echoed.

Dahti stopped and crouched in the grass, which fluttered around her in the wind.

"Where are you?" it asked again and this time, its voice was the kind of saccharine-sweet that made her teeth ache. "Surely a warrior of your strength should be willing to face me. Come out, little prophet, or I will take the villagers."

Every sense went into high alert and rage coursed through her, but she knew better than to let it lure her out immediately. She braced herself for its landing and focused on the closest wing. If she let it pass her, she could jump up and drag the frost-stave across the webbing of the appendage. It wasn't the joint, but she sensed this was the best she would be able to do.

She held her position with an effort as the dragon thudded past, then pushed herself into a sprint, vaulted upward, and struck the wing as hard as she could with her staff. She held it with both hands and twisted in the air to drag it across the fine webbing and was rewarded with a scream. At the same time, Zaara gave a distant battle cry.

The dragon pounded into a run, buffeting both women off its flanks, and lurched skyward. It climbed and spun to look at them, sculling the air. It descended a few feet, the massive wings beating unevenly.

"You have brought my vengeance down on this village forever," it hissed.

Dahti stood slowly. Fury filled her. "Your kind became too greedy," she said softly. Her voice didn't carry over the wind but she knew the dragon heard her. "And now, we see you for what you are. You reached too high, dragon."

It bellowed its rage at her and soared away, and she looked at where her arm had begun to sting. Blood poured from a long cut on her upper arm.

"Huh," she said. She was suddenly light-headed. "Well, *that* can't be good."

CHAPTER SIX

Dahti had no clear memory of the next few minutes. She recalled stumbling over the plain with Zaara beside her and how difficult it was to navigate the steep, narrow path to the mouth of the cave.

Her first real awareness was of the way the villagers drew back when the two of them arrived.

The orcs stared and the two women responded in kind. Finally, Dahti thudded heavily to her knees and the shaman hobbled forward as he called to some of the others. He looked at Zaara impersonally as if he didn't care at all that she was human.

"You, girl—you speak our tongue?"

"Yes." Zaara seemed not at all thrown by the fact that she was surrounded by orcs. "I know a little healing if you need it here."

"Any help is welcome." He knelt beside Dahti's head and placed one of his palms on each side. "I'll keep her with us while you work on that cut."

She set to work almost silently. While she had fought with easy grace, she was far more cautious with this. Her brow furrowed and she muttered things under her breath that sounded like mnemonics. The process was slow.

It worked, however. The pain began to recede as well as the light-headedness. Dahti twitched her arm experimentally and felt an ache, not the sharp pain of a cut opening once more.

"Be still," Zaara said and her voice was strained. "I am not—this is not my strength."

She complied without argument. With the combined power working in her, she felt more clear-headed with every passing moment. She remained as relaxed and motionless as she could and, when Zaara finished with a sigh, she sat. On inspection, her arm looked almost odd as if covered with blood that seemed to have come from nowhere.

"I don't suppose you care to tell me what happened," the shaman said at length. "Since I am quite sure I did not hear a god struck down."

The two combatants exchanged a look.

"We did not kill it," Dahti admitted. "We wounded it—both wings, one side, the belly, and the tail. It fled rather than stay and fight." She looked down and gathered her courage. "But it swore it would have revenge."

He sighed heavily. "Of course it did. And now it knows where our shelter is."

"You need to hide." Zaara looked up now. She was still pale from the toll her magic had taken, but she remained a confident presence. "As long as you can. I can get Dahti the training she needs to defeat the dragon, but it won't be fast."

"Oh?" He looked at her now with something approaching pity. "Do you think you can train her?"

"I didn't say that." She smiled tiredly. "I do not know the necessary spells and I cannot be away from my people for long enough to teach her. But there is a record of one fire wyrm being defeated by the water tribes. Their shamans know how."

Dahti's shoulders slumped and he looked down in despair.

"Human," he said finally, "the water tribes are no more. They were destroyed by their gods."

Zaara did not waver. "Not all of them," she said. "There are still pockets of them along the coast, and in one…" She paused. "Do your tribes fight one another?"

"No." He seemed amused. "We keep to ourselves. Our concerns—and our gods—are different."

Dahti remembered her revelation but kept quiet. This was not the time or the place.

"Then you would not strike at any water tribes," Zaara said tentatively, "even if they were powerful."

"How could they be powerful? We thought them destroyed. We thought them dead. They must be in hiding."

"They are," she agreed. "But among them still resides…Rashat."

The shaman's head came up at once. "Rashat lives?" He breathed the words. "He *lives?*"

"I know you both know who that is, but I don't," Dahti pointed out.

"Ah. Yes." Zaara gave her a tiny nod. "Rashat was the foremost among the shamans of the water tribes. He had power like nothing anyone had ever seen. They said he could conjure storms and in fact, he was noteworthy enough that humans tried to study with him." She paused. "It…it didn't go well for them."

She swallowed nervously. "Ah. So…"

"Rashat did not think well of other races," the shaman said. "As I told you, the water tribes were the most devout, and he was notable even among them. Anyone of another race who stumbled into their territory, by design or by accident, was cut down. He commanded that."

"He sounds delightful," she said brightly. "And we're glad this man is still alive because…"

"Because he's the last of the water shamans and the most powerful one they've ever seen," Zaara said bluntly before he could answer. "I was told you needed to find a way to kill a fire wyrm, and if anyone knows how, it's him." She saw the look on her face. "You seem…angry?"

"I'm merely annoyed that both you and Justin knew about the dragon before I did." She rolled her eyes moodily.

"It was such a fun revelation, though."

Dahti, aware that both her companions watched her closely, couldn't say anything to Prima in response, but she made a mental note to try to explain the concept of fun to the AI.

Zaara looked at the shaman. "Could I speak to Dahti alone?" she asked.

He hesitated before he left to return to the other orcs, all of whom had chosen to cluster on the far side of the cavern—if they remained at all. Many, it seemed, had decided to move into the caves, where they would not be subjected to the sight of a human.

Dahti was beginning to have a low opinion of some orcish beliefs.

The woman smiled at her. "Are you…from Justin's world?" she asked.

"You know about that?" she asked.

"He told me once that it was a dream," Zaara said. She smiled. "And that it wasn't real—although he seemed to change his mind on that later. He was a good friend."

"Did you know Lyle too?" she asked.

Zaara laughed at that. "Oh, yes. Lyle Stout, always the one who mucked up carefully laid plans by charging into battle. But he was a good friend as well."

"Not anymore?" Dahti asked her curiously.

"Well…" The woman sighed. "I'm training as a wizard now. I've been told I should try to shed my attachments. I'm trying but it's not easy."

"Why?" She tilted her head to the side curiously.

Zaara smiled, though she looked less happy than sad. "A wizard—if they complete their training, of course—lives for hundreds of years. No one else does. There are stories of wizards driven mad by lost love or by watching their children grow old and die. I want to help people and I can't do that if I go mad, can I?"

"I suppose not," Dahti said soberly. She swallowed. "I'm…sorry."

"Don't be." Her companion gave her an unexpectedly sunny smile. "I get to spend hundreds of years studying and protecting my village. My life will have purpose *and* pleasure." She dusted her hands briskly. "Now *you*, however, need to get to the water tribes. We must plan your route."

"I don't want his help," she said grumpily. "He sounds like a—" She almost came out with a word she'd heard one of her grandchildren say, and barely bit her tongue in time.

"He may have changed a great deal," Zaara said. "He was the most powerful and everything he did was to keep his people safe from their dragons—gods, yes? The orcs believe dragons are gods?" At her nod, she continued. "He and his tribe haven't been heard from since their gods turned on them. I would think he's probably rethought some of his beliefs."

Dahti considered this.

"You know you'll go," the woman said with a shrug.

"I beg your pardon?" She gave her an offended look. "You don't know me, young lady."

"Young lady? Who are you? My grandmother?" Zaara laughed. "Look, you aren't part of this tribe, it seems, and yet you threw yourself into danger to protect them. I'd say it's very clear you'll find Rashat and learn to destroy that dragon."

"Just because you knew Justin, you think you know all of us?" she asked.

"Oh, heavens. The first time I saw Justin, he tried to flirt with tavern wenches." The woman continued to laugh. "He did everything for fame and glory and even he turned out well. You're starting way ahead of him."

Dahti smiled despite her earlier irritation.

"I like her," Prima confided. *"She kept him on his toes too, much like Tina."*

She cleared her throat. "Ah…so you want me to waltz up to this hiding shaman and ask him for his secrets to defeat a dragon after he failed to do the same?"

"He failed to defeat a *water* dragon," Zaara said. "With water powers. You know, I'm not sure why he thought that would work. I was very surprised to learn that tribes don't exchange shamans."

"I thought the same," she agreed with a nod. "Well, then. I suppose I might as well go. Since, as you point out, I'm hardly about to let these people die because I pissed their god off. Dragon. I won't call that monster a god."

"Good," the woman said forcefully. She stood and hopped around. "Ooooooh, my leg went to sleep. Oh, dear."

Not for the first time, Dahti marveled at how realistic the game was. She nodded at her. "I'm glad you came to help. If it weren't for you…well, I would be burned to a crisp."

Zaara smiled. "It was my pleasure—truly. I enjoy studying, but I need a dose of adventure now and then. I promised my family I would do less, but I can't stand having *none.*" She reached out to shake Dahti's hand. "It was nice to meet you, Dahti. Oh! And Justin asked me to give you this."

She held out an amulet identical to the one she had worn in her incarnation as a dwarf. It would let her communicate with the team running the game and she nodded as she took it.

"If ever I can repay the favor…"

Zaara smiled. "I'm sure you will. And now, I think I will take my leave so your fellow orcs don't have to put up with a human anymore." She smiled and left, whistling a jaunty tune, and turned to call over one shoulder, "I'll get your book and leave it at the top of the hill."

"The book!" She had entirely forgotten. "Yes. Thank you."

When the woman was gone, she fastened the pendant around her neck and chewed her lip. Vengeful dragons and lost shamans. Prima had started this incarnation off with a bang.

CHAPTER SEVEN

The shaman accompanied Dahti to forage for supplies for the journey. Much to her disappointment, this seemed primarily to be root vegetables and mushrooms, the latter of which grew in abundance in the caves. They gathered the food into a basket woven from plains grasses, and he waited for her to speak.

"I'm sorry," she said finally.

He responded with a small smile but remained silent.

"My...tribe...is very strange," she told him. "We value truth and freedom over comfort. It made me angry to see the dragon preying on all of you under false pretenses. He's a tyrant and I wanted to fight him."

The shaman looked wordlessly at her.

"I shouldn't have made the decision for you," she continued. "He swore revenge on all of you, and it was because of something I did. I know it wasn't my place as I'm not a member of your tribe. So I'll fix it, I truly will. I'll free you from this god—dragon. He *isn't* a god."

He merely smiled a little secretively, which began to irritate her.

"Would you *please* say something?" she demanded.

After several moments of thought, he paused at a small stand of medium-sized mushrooms and began to pluck several tiny ones. While he might hobble, his fingers were surprisingly nimble. He showed her a palmful of them before he wrapped them in cloth.

"If you get sick, these will bring a fever down."

Dahti nodded and prayed for patience. She wanted to talk about different things than fevers and journeys.

"We are all driven by our desires and our conscience," the shaman stated finally. "And even traditions are malleable. There was a time when the tribes traveled together and we all gathered each year for a great festival. There are spells I was taught that can only have come from the air shamans."

She had no idea what to say to this so she dug another root vegetable out and looked at it glumly before she put it in the basket. Her present incarnation had significant downsides. She had never particularly enjoyed rutabagas or sweet potatoes, and that looked like most of what she was getting.

"You hope to save us," the shaman told her. He sat on his heels and looked at her, his eyes clear. She saw now that his reddish-brown skin had faint lines on it as if from very old scars. They traced his features and added an otherworldly aspect to his gaze. "It is not your actions that were at fault, earth orc. It was your motivation. We are not yours to save."

"But—" she protested.

He held up a hand. "As your elder, I claim certain privileges. One is that I ask you to think on my words during your journey instead of responding to them now."

Dahti closed her mouth. She returned to digging but a great many thoughts swirled in her head—one being that this orc was *not* her elder.

"I know very little of the water tribes from my own experience," the shaman said and changed the topic with ease. "Nevertheless, I will pass what I have heard to you. Perhaps some of it will serve you well. They live near the coast, yes, but some follow the fresh rivers and some live on the edge of the ocean, where the water is said to taste of salt."

She opened her mouth to say everyone knew that but closed it quickly. If someone were born in the plains, they might not know such a thing.

"Water is known to be the least…controllable of the elements," he said. "A wildfire may rage out of control and the earth may shake, but the force of the sea can do truly terrible things. There are stories of waves as tall as mountains."

Reflexively, she shuddered. "I have heard the same stories."

He nodded. "Their shamans do not use rapid magic," he said. "Like a wave, their magic gathers slowly and works, finally, with great power and unstoppable force—or it works like water wearing away at the stone with tiny touches that each weaken so slightly that one cannot think of them as doing damage at all. To command the power of water is a strange thing for a mortal."

Dahti nodded. "To use such a slow power against a dragon—"

"You keep using that word."

"It is the word the other races have for the beings you call gods. When we speak of gods, we speak of something quite different—without human form, usually. I mean, physical form." She kept forgetting she wasn't human any longer.

"You know a great deal about the humans," the shaman said mildly.

She tried to find a suitable lie, could not, and decided to not say anything at all.

He sighed. "I wish you would tell me the truth of your past, child."

The answer came to her in sudden clarity. She grinned impishly at him. "How old are you, grandfather? Because I'm eighty-four." At the widening of his eyes, she laughed. "And, as *your* elder, I claim certain privileges—like not having to answer those questions."

He threw his head back and laughed. "Ah, so you claim to be the eldest in the tribe? An interesting thing to hear from one in a strong body."

"Truth is stranger than fiction," she said serenely. "I was called to this place without knowing why but now, I think it is to free you from a false god."

"Is that so?" He stood and hefted his basket. "There is enough here to keep you for a week or more on the road and after that, I must ask that you forage as you go. Our people need all the supplies they can get."

"Then I'll take only half of this," Dahti said at once. "I've put you in enough danger."

They walked to the main caves while he told her what else he knew of the water tribes. They had banded together when their gods woke, he claimed, and had therefore been together when they were all struck down.

"What of Rashat?" she asked him.

"Rashat…" He sighed. "I both envy you your chance to study with him, earth orc, and pity you. It is said he was a most unlovable man."

"That seems accurate." She would, quite frankly, have been shocked if a man who murdered lost travelers was friendly and jovial.

"We heard about him even before he was a shaman. His coming was told in the stars—even to our people. We sent emissaries, in fact, to learn what those stars meant, and were told of an infant who could summon water and play with it from the very day of his birth. He used magic as naturally as he breathed. Perhaps…"

"Perhaps?" Dahti prompted when the words trailed away.

"Perhaps that is why he clung so hard to the ways of his people," the shaman said contemplatively. "What else could they teach him? The magic he used was beyond that of his elders. For a certainty, they could teach him the ways of water, but the traditions were the only thing they had that he was not born with." He shrugged.

"You said they were wiped out," she said after a moment. "How did you learn of that if you thought all of them were dead?"

"The air tribes sent word." He shook his head. "So rarely do they speak to the rest of us… But they said they saw the god rise out of the ocean, taller than the tallest wave, slow and deadly, and that after the attack, they never again saw the water tribes stir along the coast. Nor did we see their travelers in caravans or receive word. I was newly apprenticed when word came. Rashat would have been…oh, a few years older than I was."

Dahti looked curiously at him.

"Do you resent him?"

"Rashat?" He looked at her. "Why?"

"I think you know why."

He smiled. "Then the answer would be yes, I do. Or, rather, I envy him, even though I understand how foolish it is to do so."

"Why would you say it's foolish?" She smiled at his sheepishness.

"What is the point in wishing for such magic?" the shaman asked. "No amount of wishing can change the past. I was not born summoning fire as Rashat summoned water. Tales of my skill will never be told to children of the tribe. There is no help for that."

Dahti looked sympathetically at him. She could hear the ache in his voice and she recognized it because she had seen it in every single person she knew, as well as herself.

"And it brought him no joy," the shaman said heavily. "In the end, his skill did not help him or his tribe. I imagine he is a broken man now. You will have your work cut out for you, young one—or elder, whichever you may be." The gleam of a smile told her he remembered her assertion of being eighty-four.

She took a gamble and planted the seed. "Shaman." She put a hand out to stop him before they reached the main cavern. "Do you remember what Zaara said—the human? She said only one record existed of a fire wyrm being defeated and that it had been defeated by a *water* shaman."

"Yes, but even their magic did not help them when—"

"What if it wasn't his skill or the amount of magic he had?" she pressed. "What if water magic cannot defeat a water god? What if *you* and *your* line might have defeated that god, the same way his line once helped your people?"

The shaman stared at her.

"You said the tribes once came together each year for a festival," she reminded him. "What if there was a time when the shamans shared their spells?"

"I…" His voice trailed away.

"I'm no proper orc," she said frankly. "You and I both know it. But I think the freedom of your people lies in your unity. Share your ways—your dances, your goods, your livestock…and your magic. Restart the festival." She grasped his hand urgently. "I will make what I did right, but think on that while I am gone."

He smiled at her. "I will. You, however—you think on what I said."

"That it is not my actions that were at fault but my motivations," Dahti quoted. "That you are not mine to save. I remember."

"Good." He patted her arm. "Go now. I am an old man and I have earned one more privilege."

"Oh?"

"Yes. Not having to grow too fond of people who may die violently. I sense you may be one of them. Run along now." He ushered her briskly through the main cave as she laughed.

"Do you find that funny?" Prima questioned.

"It *is* funny," she said as she made her way up the steep path. "It's called black humor."

"I do not understand humans at all."

"Yes, but we knew that, right?"

"I suppose," the AI said glumly, and she laughed again.

"Cheer up. Most of the time, humans don't understand each other either. You're not doing any worse than a normal human would."

"Oh, that's comforting."

"Don't be snide." Dahti reached the top of the hill and saw her book—as well as a scroll. "What's this?" She knelt and broke the wax seal—an ornate Z—before she stretched it open.

It was a gorgeous map, the kind that reminded her why maps had once been so prized. Each line was painstakingly drawn by hand, forests and deserts were rendered in lush washes of color, and tiny cities were highlighted with distinctive drawings. She recognized both Berghold and Insea on sight.

The mountain of the fire dragon was marked clearly, as well as the little village, and a small star along the coast indicated the last known position of the water tribe. It was, she estimated, a little way inland along a river.

Judging by the distance between Berghold and Insea, which had taken two weeks by cart, her walk would take a week and a half if she set a brisk pace.

"You'll have more than enough time to practice your magic," Prima said with satisfaction.

"I should have known you'd get me to do this again," Dahti said wryly.

"You're a natural. Even the other humans say so. Besides, I'll arrange for company on the way."

"And does that mean friends or attacks?" She rolled the map and put it in her makeshift pack. "Prima? I asked, does that mean friends or enemies? Prima?"

Unsurprisingly, no answer was forthcoming.

She sighed and put her pack on. It was halfway through the day, by her estimation, and she might as well begin walking into whatever trap Prima had planned for her.

CHAPTER EIGHT

The rest of the day was entirely uneventful, which only annoyed Dahti more with each step she took.

And there were far too many steps.

She wasn't sure if Prima was tormenting her or giving her time to recover, but she suspected it was the former. By dinnertime, she was famished and sore. She took time to set out the mushrooms, cup up, the way the shaman had taught her so that they would collect morning dew, and chose a position under an acacia tree so she could take water from the leaves in the morning.

With her chores, such as they were completed, she sat and read. There wasn't much to do otherwise, and as much as she instinctively feared magic, she also greatly enjoyed it. She wasn't sure that any of the spells in this book would do her any good, but at least practicing magic in general would help. It seemed that with each level she attained in her Spellcasting skill, she received extra points on her magic bar.

Her practice began with a few repetitions of earth-shock, a spell that encased something in what looked like dried mud and shattered it from the inside out. She didn't have to have an actual target and so she spent time making balls of mud in midair that thudded to the ground and shattered there.

The next iteration of the skill was stone-shock, which harnessed the quick-moving power of stones. She had to read that twice to make sure she had seen it correctly, but there was no mistaking the text. Roughly-drawn illustrations were provided of places where stone stabbed through the earth like a spear or where it had cracked apart from an earthquake. It was this schism—similar to cracking mud and yet far stronger—that she would harness with stone-shock.

To have something to focus on, she shaped a little mound of dirt and attempted the spell several times.

Every time, it took her magic but nothing happened to the dirt.

"Prima," she called finally, "is it not working because I'm trying earth magic on a mound of dirt?"

"No."

"Does that mean it *is* the problem or it *isn't?*"

"It is not the problem," Prima said, amused. *"It wouldn't harm the dirt but if you were doing it correctly, it would still work."*

"Blast." Dahti sighed. She took a moment to read the instructions again and muttered the phrases aloud. "…stabs up through the dirt…strong even in the face of the wind…" She considered what she'd read. When she tried to meld her feelings about earth and stone and the strong, slow face of a mountain with the speed of a blade, nothing came to her.

Instead, this time, she pictured the scene the book described —a piece of rock that had once thrust through the dirt with astounding force but which now sat implacably in the blazing sun and whistling wind.

The power left her with a shudder and her eyes snapped open. A spur of rock protruded through her mound of dirt. A moment later, all of it cracked and crumbled.

"Ha," she said with great satisfaction.

That, unfortunately, had been the last of her magic, and she knew it would take time to replenish. She took another sip of water and swirled it in her mouth before she swallowed, then lay under the tree.

Now that the sun had set, it was chilly and she realized she should have asked the shaman for a blanket. She only had the cloth from the book, so she tucked that around her shoulders and curled into a ball under the leafy canopy.

Her last journey, she thought grumpily, had been one of ample food and nice, soft bedrolls under thick blankets. There had been ale and sausages heated over an open flame. She'd enjoyed little red apples, freshly baked bread with thick slabs of soft cheese, brown-sugar cured ham…

She drifted off to sleep with her mouth watering and dreamed of featherbeds and tables groaning under heavy platters of food.

Justin climbed out of the taxi and sighed. Behind him, Tina slid out as well and shut the door. The driver helped her to unload the bags while her friend stood and thought gloomily about how useless he was these days.

She thanked the man and turned to see his face.

"It'll get better," she assured him. "Two weeks ago, you could barely walk from one side of the room to the other, and now look at you."

He shrugged grumpily, took the rolling suitcase, and set off. Unfortunately, he couldn't dodge the fast-walking New Yorkers as quickly as they seemed to want him to, and within a few meters, he was already both exhausted and annoyed.

"Oh, yeah?" Tina called to someone who had shouted at them. "Well, up yours, too!"

"Tina," he said, pained.

"And *you*—oh, wait, sorry. I was in insult mode. Never mind.

You, I like." She slid her arm around his waist, both a sweet gesture and a helpful one as he could lean against her.

With a laugh, he waited for her to precede him through the revolving door. Instead, one of the side doors opened and Nick stepped out.

"I thought I saw you," he panted. Clearly, he had run upstairs. "I only now got your text about heading here from the airport. We meant to bring you a wheelchair—"

"I do *not* need a wheelchair," he said hotly.

"Yes, he does," Tina contradicted. She squeezed his side. "However much damage it does to your masculinity to have trouble walking after months in a coma, I promised your parents I wouldn't let you keel over on the sidewalk anywhere. Into that chair, mister."

Justin grumbled and sat in the wheelchair Nick had ready inside the doors. After even the brief walk from the taxi—although, he supposed, there had also been the airport and plane to navigate—he wanted nothing more than to curl in a ball and sleep.

"Your doctor sent your most recent reports," the engineer told him as he pushed the wheelchair through security. "It seems your stamina is off the charts."

"Yes—the bottom end."

Nick laughed. "The top end, thank you very much. Now, I hear how hard you've worked to recover, but I like to think all the low-grade muscle activation you did in the pod helped."

"He did mention that." He leaned his chin on one hand as the chair wheeled into an elevator. It was horrifying to think of how much worse things might be if he'd experienced normal atrophy during his coma.

In the lab, he was greeted by several assistants he recognized as well as DuBois, the eccentric doctor who had pioneered the early stages of PIVOT's treatment. The man gave him a somewhat sticky handshake and the reason for it became clear when he clapped the same hand on his shoulder and gestured with the other for him to help himself to a big bowl of cheese-and-caramel popcorn.

Justin stifled a laugh but still took a handful. One of the benefits of recovering from a coma was that you could get away with things like junk food.

"So, is Dotty back in the game?" he asked around a mouthful of popcorn.

"Oh, God, he's made another convert." Amber's voice cut through his mumbles. She stared at his full mouth and cheese-dust-stained hand with amusement. "I swear, Diatek Industries will prop up the Chicago Mix industry singlehandedly soon. Hello, Justin. Hi, Tina."

"Hi." Tina waved.

"How was your trip?"

"How is any plane trip?" the woman asked with a shrug. "Gross. Bad food."

"I liked it." Justin smiled tiredly. "I haven't been out of the house in weeks except to go into the game briefly in the California offices. This is kind of nice. I always wanted to see New York. Of course, I always assumed I'd be able to walk more than a block when I got here."

"This is the perfect time for a horse-drawn carriage," Amber suggested.

"Oooh." Tina's face lit up.

He filed that away for later. His relationship with Tina had been a strange one, beginning on the same night they had the car accident that left him comatose. When they reconnected, it had been in the virtual world of PIVOT, and she had helped him to prepare to wake from his coma.

Since then, she had been a strange fixture in his life—although the two of them steadfastly avoided talking about exactly what their relationship *was*.

For his part, he began to realize he'd caught serious feelings, and the way her face lit up at the idea of a horse-drawn carriage made him think he might have a way to impress her. His mind drifted for a few pleasant moments until someone cleared their throat meaningfully.

"What? I wasn't—never mind." He shook his head several times. "Sorry. You were saying?"

"We were saying that Dotty has several solo days on her journey. She had a few choices, technically, including bringing someone from the orc village with her, but she decided to go alone. We thought it might be good if you showed up to speak to her and give her a chance to reflect. Frankly, one of the features of the game is its social qualities." Amber shrugged. "It's generally not good for people to be completely without that."

"Ooooh, could I go?" Tina hopped from one foot to the other. "Please, please, please?"

"You?" Justin raised an eyebrow. "You didn't cause enough diplomatic trouble in Berghold so now, you want to start an all-out war with the orcs?"

"For the last time, those fuckers started it." She jabbed a finger at him. "All with their fancy hats and shady dice rolls. I know what they were up to, and it was nothing good, I'll tell you that."

He rolled his eyes.

"And I won't cause a war," she pointed out, "because this is Dotty, who is a human and knows I'm another human. Real person."

"*That's* why you want to cause a war?"

"So, can I?" Tina begged Amber.

Justin had been confident that the others wouldn't agree but to his horror, they seemed to seriously consider it.

"It would be more advantageous to your recovery if we keep you out of the game for now," Amber said to him.

"Wait, what?"

"And we'd have more time for the promo shoots," Nick agreed. Part of the reason for the trip had been to shoot video of

Justin, along with more interviews that Diatek and PIVOT could use for promotional materials. They weren't lacking new test subjects but wanted to accrue as much public goodwill as possible to counteract the nasty rumors being spread online.

Some people *really* didn't like the idea of a virtual reality.

"I think that makes more sense," Amber said.

He sighed glumly.

"What about this?" she suggested gently. "We can give the two of you a lovely date in Insea later tonight. It will limit your time in-game, which will be good for you, but you'll still get to have a good time while you're here. We can maybe even throw in a dragon ride."

Justin brightened immediately. "That sounds good."

"Excellent. In that case, we'll get you to the photoshoot set and Tina, you come with me and we'll get all your patches on to get you into the game."

***

Dahti trudged along on the fourth day, whistling Mack the Knife to herself, when she first noticed the other orc. A jolt spiked through her. Tall and hulking, the man had tattoos across his bare chest and arms, and his head was shaved apart from a long ponytail at the very top of his head. His tusks were long, and his skin was the same deep red-brown as the other fire orcs.

"Here we go, huh, Prima?"

"Mmm," the AI said noncommittally.

"What does that mean?" she asked under her breath. She tightened her hold on her stave and strode forward.

A cheery wave and an excited, "Hi!" left her confused.

She stopped dead in her tracks. "Er…hi?" Of all the things she expected from a muscular and imposing orc, this was not one of them.

"It's Tina!" the orc said excitedly in the same deep, booming voice. "Justin's girlfriend. Friend. Thing. Anyway, hi."

"The one I last saw in Berghold?" she asked quizzically.

"Yeah." The orc smashed one fist into the other palm. "Lemme tell you, those two dwarves still got it coming for that. Maybe I'll go there next."

"I'd change bodies first," she said, amused.

"Nah, I *like* this one. I'm so strong! And tall! Also, I've always wondered what it would be like to go topless. This is nice."

Dahti snorted.

"Anyway, I'm simply here to walk with you," Tina said. "They thought you might want company."

"Oh. Thank you very much."

"Also, I can carry things now." She made her muscular avatar flex several times in deeply exaggerated ways.

With a snort, she handed over her pack and stave. "After four days of walking, I'm not too proud to take that offer. Also, it will help me hunt."

"You hunt?" Tina asked with great interest.

"Do you see any grocery stores?"

"Well…no. But I didn't have to do anything like that when I was in the game last time. I merely wandered around Insea and competed in the tournament." She looked at the mountains a few miles away. "Will you simply go straight over? They don't look very…what's the word…"

"Good for my health?" Dahti suggested. "From what I understand, there's a passage of some kind that only the orcs can find. I hope it works off appearance and not knowledge because otherwise, I'll have a bad time of it."

The grass rustled nearby and she stopped her companion with a hand on her arm. She crept forward, holding her breath and magic at the ready.

The rabbit did an about-face almost as quickly as it had hopped out of the grass, but she was prepared. Her spell caught it on the head, something she'd learned to do after she lost several meals to ill-placed spells.

It was difficult to eat an animal when the entire carcass had crumbled into chunks of dirt.

"*Aha*," she said in satisfaction. "Finally, a good meal. There's only so long I can live on sweet potatoes and mushrooms."

"I don't know, with a nice steak—"

"Do you see any nice steaks? Or bottles of red wine? Or loaves of garlic bread?" Dahti raised an eyebrow.

"Bleh. You should see if they can restart your game in Insea. It's much nicer there."

She smiled. "I'll consider that for next time—right now, I'm afraid, I have a village to save." While they walked, she explained the story. The sun went behind the mountains quite early and cast welcome shadows onto their path.

Tina's presence was a pleasant diversion, she reflected. The days had been filled with magic practice and snarky comments from Prima, as well as a fair amount of introspection, but that grew old very quickly. There wasn't even a radio for a musical interlude.

Her new companion, on the other hand, was a wild mix of irreverent and humorous who always attempted things like leaping onto rocks to balance one-footed. Dahti was relatively sure she would strangle the woman if she had to take the entire journey with her but as a diversion, it was pleasant.

"So, did you meet Zaara?" she called to her at one point.

"I did." She laughed. "I think Justin had a little crush on her. He always gets all blustery when she comes up in conversation. She helped him on his first missions—her and Lyle."

"And then you and Lyle fought with him in Insea," she said and put the timeline together in her head.

"That's right." Tina wobbled on a rock and hopped down. "You do magic too, right? I chose the daggers because the leather armor was killer but *man*, did it chafe."

Prima snickered in her head. *"You should have seen her trying to walk after her first match."*

She shook her head with a grin. "Something to remember. The robes the magicians wear are much more comfortable—although I discovered I prefer to have some combat skills as well as magic."

"The best of both worlds," the woman agreed. "Whoops, I'm getting a beep. It's time to leave. Is there anything you need before I go?"

"Mmm. I don't think so. I have my amulet, anyway, so I can contact them if there's anything I *do* need. Although…I don't suppose Justin has any contacts among the water orcs?"

"I don't think so," Tina said.

"Really? He seems to know important people everywhere."

"Ah, that's a misconception—you've simply met both of the people he knew, that's all." She laughed. "Well, if there's anything, let me know. I'd arrange for a care package at your next campsite, but I have a feeling your choices and mine might be a little different. That is, unless you *do* like tequila and nachos."

"Young lady," Dahti said, "*everyone* likes tequila and nachos."

"Oh, hot damn. I knew I liked you. I'll arrange for those, then." Tina gave her a mock-salute, twirled—an especially excellent sight with her avatar's tall, muscle-bound frame—and disappeared in a shower of sparkles.

"The sparkles were a nice touch," she told Prima.

"I thought so. And I don't know how she thought she was going to get the tequila and nachos to you, but I'll arrange for them."

CHAPTER NINE

By the time Justin finished his briefings and headshots for the coming interviews, he was exhausted. Even talking and focusing took considerable effort these days.

Jacob noticed his frustration and smiled sympathetically. "I can't imagine what this must feel like."

"It takes so much effort simply to get through the *day*," he told him but managed a smile. "But, hey—I'm walking, I'm up and about, and I'm not still stuck in a hospital. I think I'd be going insane if I was."

The other man grinned. "Nah, we'd simply swoop in and give you a crazy, dragon-riding adventure. Speaking of which…" He gestured to the door. "I'm told there's a very romantic date set up for you and Tina."

"*Date?*" he spluttered.

Jacob froze. "Amber said date."

He thought back to the conversation in the lab. Amber *had* said that, he realized in horror. Not that the thought of a date was horrifying, of course, but he had blithely agreed to the idea of a date without even thinking to ask Tina if they were still going out.

"Are you and Tina *not* dating?" his companion asked with real confusion.

"That's the thing," he confessed. "I don't know. I have no idea."

"You…came out together." Jacob set the wheelchair up and darted him a look, one eyebrow raised. "And walked in here with your arms around each other. And weren't you two dating before all this?"

"We went on *a* date," he said. "One! And then we've…hung out…since then. Okay, and there's been some cuddling. She comes over often. I see her every day but I don't want to presume that—"

"Justin," Jacob said seriously. "I went to MIT, so I want you to know that what I'm about to say comes from a place of great expertise. I spent *years* surrounded by some of the absolutely *worst* flirters in the world. I mean, these people were *terrible* at relationships. Incredibly bad. Comically bad. Justin, my man— you are off-the-charts terrible at this."

He spluttered.

"I mean it," the man told him. "I see the way you two look at each other. You hang out every day. You cuddle. She came out here with you. You had all those good talks in the game. Neither of you objected when Amber said she would set you up a date. Justin, my man, you two are *dating.*"

Justin sat hard in the wheelchair. "Oh, God."

"You sit there and process while I'll get you downstairs," Jacob said. "You know, for your date." He added, somewhat wickedly, "Oh, and don't worry—we've set up some alerts in case there's any equipment stuff, but we'll all make sure to be elsewhere so you can have some…" He paused for dramatic effect. "Privacy," he finished blandly.

"If I weren't recovering from a coma, I'd beat you to a pulp," he said grumpily.

"Out of curiosity, how would you say your skill at fighting compares to your skill at relationships?"

"I will fucking kill you. Until you die from it." He lowered his face into his hands as the wheelchair jolted into the lab.

"What's going on?" Amber asked. "Is he okay?"

"Absolutely," Jacob said smoothly, although a trace of laughter still lingered in his voice. "He's merely contemplating his—"

"I will kill you," Justin said again as he raised his head.

"Well, you wouldn't be the first one to want to try," she said cheerfully. She opened the lid of the pod and saw the look on his face. "He and I used to date."

"See?" Jacob said. "I know what I'm talking about."

Despite his discomfort, Justin laughed and summoned his energy to get into the pod and tried not to fall asleep while they hooked him up. He was surprised by how much he was both looking forward to re-entering the game and dreading it. Returning to help Dotty had been one thing. He'd had a purpose and he could put most of his feelings behind him to assume his role as a guide and mentor.

But going back in simply as Justin was somehow different.

Not to mention that the idea of what he would say to Tina made him break out in a cold sweat.

"Count back from ten," Amber told him.

"Ten…nine…"

The game took hold quickly now that he was used to it. He opened his eyes to the familiar view of Insea. He was in a little alley, although a clean one, lit with lights that were suspended all around him in midair. He looked down at a nice shirt and pants and nodded, satisfied that at least he looked okay.

Well, he was dressed well. The rest of it was simply what it was.

He could hear the music of a harp from down the alley and could smell delicious food as well. Justin walked slowly, his heart pounding in his chest.

A date. This is an actual date.

When he entered the courtyard, his jaw dropped. Amber had

not been kidding about the romantic date. The food spread on the table was not only mouth-watering, it was gorgeously arranged around centerpieces and candles. A pergola across the courtyard had vines twined all around it, covered in lush greenery and tiny white flowers. A fountain nearby caught the light of the fairy lanterns.

Everything was perfect.

Justin turned and found a sudden rush of courage. "Tina, I need to say something—" He broke off with an undignified squeak.

"Hi," boomed the giant, hulking orc. He had tusks and war tattoos all across one side of his chest...and he wore a fancy, drapey silk dress.

"Um..." He couldn't seem to think of a single word and could hear the AI laughing hysterically in his head. "I'm so sorry— wrong courtyard—"

The orc wavered in front of his eyes, transformed into Tina, and doubled over with laughter. She held her hand over her mouth as she gasped for air. "Oh, man, your *face*—"

Justin sent a silent prayer heavenward that Jacob had been serious about not watching them while they were on the date.

She was still laughing as she moved closer to take his hand. "I'm so sorry. I had that avatar to go see Dotty, and then I thought it would be funny for you to arrive and see it—especially when I saw the dress." She hesitated, suddenly shy, and looked down at it.

"You look beautiful," he told her honestly.

"That's nice, but I'm not beautiful." She gestured at her tattoos and her short frame. "At best, I'm pretty."

"I'm—I don't think—I'm confused." He thought about the lost and aimless person he'd been on their first date, then remembered defeating Sephith and the demon and winning in the arena. He squared his shoulders. "I think the dress suits you, and you…well, you took my breath away in it with both avatars. But for different reasons, of course."

Tina responded with a peal of laughter, then looked curiously at him. "You seem…"

Justin waited. He wasn't sure what to say.

After a moment, she shrugged. "Different, but I'm not sure how. Is everything okay?"

"Yes," he said with certainty. He took her hand. "Do you want to eat?"

"Mmm, maybe in a while." She looked to where couches stood near the fountain, with glasses of wine and various appetizers nearby. "I…well, I wanted to talk to you about something. I probably didn't make the best start with the orc avatar."

He stopped to stare at her. "Are we *both* horrible at this?"

"What? Wait, what am I horrible at?"

"Nothing! Not—I didn't mean—" He waved his hands. "Jacob said—"

"Jacob said *what*?" Tina asked.

Oh, dear. He gulped.

"This should be fun," the AI commented.

"Would you give us a moment?" he asked her.

"I can't. I am literally running this world."

Justin sighed. To Tina, he said, "Jacob asked how things were going with us. And, uh…I explained that I wasn't sure how to talk to you about it, and he said I was being ridiculous, and that we were probably…I mean—ohhhh, he was right. I'm so bad at this."

She went to get him a glass of wine. "Drink up. Liquid courage. Not that we can get drunk here, of course, but maybe it'll work as a placebo."

"Maybe it will." He drained it in a gulp. "Okay, here it is. I really like you." His face burned but he pressed on. "You make me laugh and you also make me want to live a good life for myself. You were the first person who ever asked me what *I* wanted, not because you assumed I wanted to be rich and successful but because you wondered what would make me happy. I mean…it's not about the things you do. Why I like you, that is. It's because you're you. And when I look at you…" He shook his head, a little lost for words now. "Maybe we're already dating or maybe you thought we were only friends. But I'd like…well, I'd like to be dating. If you want."

He blew a breath out. No one would want to go out with a dude who stumbled over the words that way. Especially someone covered in tattoos who liked skinny-dipping and pissing her parents off.

"I'm glad I went on that first date," Tina said.

Justin looked up. She met his gaze briefly, then focused on her glass of wine. Her fingers were white-knuckled around it.

"Honestly, it's been hard," she said. "I said so much to you about doing stuff for *yourself* and all that but I was doing the same thing you were. I merely tried to piss my parents off. I hadn't ever honestly thought about doing what I wanted to do, and I still don't know what I want to do. You—you have this career, you already had your video game channel, and you were going for things. I never was."

She downed her wine and poured herself another glass. Her hands shook so hard that some splashed onto the floor.

"And then I nearly killed you," she said. "I felt like I ruined your life and I put your whole family through something they should have never had to go through and—no, *please* don't argue, Justin. You know it's true. And I wanted to help. I wanted to do anything I could to make it right and I wanted you and your parents to hate me because at least then, the world would make sense.

"But you wouldn't. You didn't hate me, and we tried to get you back into the real world and then you've been recovering. I kept telling myself I didn't know what I felt and you didn't know what *you* felt and I couldn't ambush your recovery by—"

"Hey." Justin put her wine glass on the table and took her hands in his.

She took a deep breath. "I've wanted to ask you what we were this whole time. And yesterday, Amber said she'd make us a date and you didn't even blink. You simply agreed, and I felt like I was walking on *air*, Justin."

He laughed and squeezed his eyes shut. "I didn't realize until just before this that she'd said that. It was why Jacob was talking to me about it. I panicked about whether or not you thought I was being presumptuous."

Tina started to laugh. She laughed like she wasn't entirely sure she could stop and after a moment, he wrapped his arms around her. Hers came around him as well, and she squeezed so tightly that he made an undignified noise and tapped on her shoulder.

"Excuse me. I need to breathe."

She responded with a sniffle and a laugh. "So, are we…"

"Dating? I think so." he looked at her. They were too different in height to lean their foreheads together easily. "Unless we have to have it notarized or something."

"I'm a notary."

Tina must have heard that too because she snorted and looked up. She looked over her shoulder at the wine and the appetizers. "How about we have good food and appreciate everything Prima put out for us?"

"Thank you," the AI said and sounded pleased.

"Oh, right—Prima is what Dotty named it?"

"Prima is what I named myself, thank you very much. None of the rest of you bothered to ask if I had a name."

"Right." He cleared his throat and tried to assess the risk of a robot uprising. "Thank you, Prima."

"You're welcome. I'll give you two some privacy."

Justin sat on one of the couches and sighed happily as he popped an appetizer into his mouth. "Mmf. Amazing. Melted cheese is the best appetizer. You can't change my mind."

"Almost every culture has something like fried balls of cheese. And the rest…" Tina shook her head. "We need to find all of them and wander around with platters of mozzarella sticks or something. This is so good."

"Let's see how it goes with the wine." He poured more into his glass and handed Tina hers again. He took a sip. "Mmm. Pear. Oak. Berries."

"I didn't know you knew about wine," she said in surprise.

"I don't. I was bullshitting."

She snorted wine up her nose and wiped it with a napkin. "Oh, man, so this game makes it sting when you get stuff up your nose. That's impressive, but also—ow." She took a cautious sip of the wine. "How am I supposed to do this?"

"I think you're supposed to kind of roll it over the sides and back of your tongue, with the very front of your mouth open."

"Thith feelth ridiculouth."

"Nah, it'th vewy clathy." Justin swallowed. "As you can tell, this is a fine vintage. And how do I know, you ask?" He held a finger up, popped a mouthful of melted cheese in his mouth, and took a sip of wine. "It goes well with the melted cheese. That's the only wine metric that matters."

Tina laughed. "See, we should do this more often."

"We can do it again tonight," he suggested. "Have a real-world date after this one. There has to be somewhere we can find melted cheese in New York City."

"Probably," she agreed. "On the other hand—and hear me out —room service."

Justin clinked her glass with his. "I like the way you think."

CHAPTER TEN

Despite her concerns, the tunnel through the mountain was unprotected by any magic at all. It was exactly where the map put it, and Dahti suspected that the "magic" was simply that no one else knew it was there. Most people didn't travel in the orc lands to start with.

About halfway through the mountain, when she could not see light on either side but *could* hear the occasional creak and shift of earth, she realized there was likely significant magic involved in keeping it from collapsing.

At least she hoped there was.

She tried to feel for it as she walked. During her time in the world, she had studied various forms of magic, so did that mean she could sense other people's spells? She searched for the feeling she had when she created little spurs of rock or even clouds of dust.

Perplexingly, she couldn't discern any spells at all. This tunnel was, somehow, impossibly stable despite the fact that it existed deep within a mountain. Not so much as a piece of dust shook loose when the rock shifted and settled above her. But, try as she might, she couldn't sense a spell.

A few minutes of concentrated thought finally told her why.

It was roughly the same reason that a person in Zabar's couldn't "see" New York City—the spell was *massive*. She walked with her mouth hanging open in awe. Her progress had been fairly good with small spells—the kind that could trap a wolf's paw or distract an elven battle eagle—but everything she'd achieved was insignificant compared to the scale of this.

Utterly fascinated, she hoped she stayed in the game long enough to make something of this magnitude.

Dahti was so absorbed in the beauty of it and the power that threaded in faint lines through the rock above her that she hardly noticed the first glimmers of light. In fact, it was the scent of salt that caught her attention first. She was still a fair distance from the coast, but the air in this part of the tunnel was fresher and it smelled unmistakably of the ocean.

She walked gladly toward it, both pleased to be out in the open and sad to leave this marvel of earth magic behind her. She had to remember to send Lyle a letter, she thought, so dwarven wizards could come to examine it. Surely they and the earth shamans would have much to discuss.

Then again, the races didn't seem to be on the best of terms.

Her first step out of the tunnel was into a paradise. She gasped and looked at the sweep of the sea, entirely different from the North Atlantic coast. The water wasn't iron-gray and white-capped. It was such a deep blue that she could hardly believe her eyes.

White sand beaches were flanked on one side by reefs filled with shoals of quick-darting fish and on the other side by verdant forests. A stream wound through the trees, catching the sunlight, and spilled out over a tumble of rocks and into the sea.

Dahti's gaze traced the glint of the river through the trees and she thought she saw a rustle of movement. It was difficult to tell from this distance if what she saw was orcs or something else—a large cat, perhaps—and she considered how best to find out without getting mauled when she noticed something else that was very important.

Several spears were pointed at her.

She looked around cautiously. The gathered orcs, gray-skinned with a distinctive bluish tint, stared in return.

"Hello," she said with no better ideas.

"Explain your presence, *earth orc.*" One of them—she hadn't seen which—all but spat the words. When she tried to determine who had spoken, the warrior jabbed a spear at her. "I said—"

"I heard you," she snapped.

The tips of the spears moved much closer.

"Damn," she muttered. When nothing else came to mind, she put her hands up and tried not to show her exasperation while she studied them. "I am here to learn magic." When no one said anything, she added, "May I say that the fire tribes are glad to learn that your people still live?"

"The fire tribes?" one of them asked.

"She came out of fire territory," another said. He curled his lip. "So you told them we still lived. How long have the earth tribes known and not sent help?"

"My tribe was taken by illness," Dahti said. She hoped this tribe thought the same way the last one had or she was about to be an orc kebab. "I found shelter with a fire village and while I was there, we learned that you still lived."

"How?"

"From..." Oh, this was awkward. "From a human."

"Do you expect us to believe that?" the first one asked harshly. She stared at her with an expression of deep disgust. "A lone earth orc traipses out of fire territory and claims she learned our tribe was still alive from a human. And what was it you said? You're here to learn *magic*?"

"Truth is stranger than fiction," she responded. That would have to be her go-to phrase for a while, she suspected.

"Heh." The orc gave her an appreciative smile. "You lie well, earth orc. But you'll still die here."

"Ah." It seemed her appreciation was the kind one warrior gave another before an honorable death. She sighed. "Perhaps I could ask that your shaman be allowed to assess whether I am lying or not?"

A very long pause followed. Several of them looked at each other, much like they were having a secret conversation they'd had several times before. Eventually, the leader directed two of them to put their spears up and withdrew with the others for a whispered conversation.

"And yes," Dahti called, "I know your shaman is Rashat."

Everyone gave her a sharp look. The whispered conversation became more intense and included a great deal of hand-waving.

Finally, their leader returned, her spear at the ready. "Why do you want to learn magic from Rashat? Talk."

Dahti had, thankfully, spent several days practicing this exact speech. There hadn't been much else to do, after all. She'd intended to give it to Rashat, of course, but she could modify it because she knew it by heart at this point.

"The fire village I sheltered with has been attacked by its god," she said evenly. "Since word reached us of the water tribes' destruction, many orcs have wondered if the gods are just—and if they are worthy of the sacrifices they demand. When their god came, they stood against him for the first time, and although we drove him back, he has sworn to have his revenge. Only one tribe has ever defeated a fire god and that is the water tribe. We thought there was no hope, but if Rashat still lives, perhaps he can train me."

None of them said anything but it was clear that she had struck a nerve.

It was also not difficult to see their mood and it was one of heartbreak and pity. The leader put her spear up quietly and the others followed.

"Is Rashat dead?" Dahti asked.

"No," the warrior said heavily. "But he will not train you."

"I know there have been differences between the tribes," she said urgently. "I know he may doubt my commitment or my faith, and he is free to doubt it as much as he wishes. I will do anything. I will promise whatever I must promise, if only he will help that village. There are children there, little ones who have never done anything wrong, and they need his help. Surely they do not deserve to die as sacrifices to a fire god." She stopped when the leader held a hand up.

"It is…not that." She gestured to a rocky outcropping nearby. "Come, sit. I will tell you the story. Then maybe you will understand."

Dahti dropped her pack and her staff and sat where indicated. It was precarious up there on the edge of a towering cliff that must be at least as high as the Eiffel Tower, if not higher. The view of the sea showed a huge bay and beyond it, a series of small islands rising out of the water.

"The elders say they saw the god take the islands first," the warrior explained. "For two days, they saw the beast flying and touching down. They heard the sounds of celebrations and sacrifice on the winds—and then they heard screams. The god was not appeased even though it had taken everything."

She said nothing but her heart clenched. All too well, she remembered the screams of the villagers as they fled across the plains.

"It had been many generations since the gods had come to us," the leader explained. "More than twenty. The elders were devout. They had made their offerings each year into the sea—the freshest fish, the choicest crops. They said the prayers and burned incense. Warriors were sent out into the deep ocean in boats to be claimed if the god wanted. They had never taken more than the sea could give and had never taken it for granted. And still, it was not enough."

Dahti looked at her with what she hoped was encouragement.

The woman smiled slightly. "It aches to tell the story, even though I was not there for it. My grandparents told me only once, but I remember every word. They trusted their god completely and it betrayed them. The pain I feel when I speak the story is not mine, but theirs."

She recalled her grandparents speaking of the great war, of the plague that had killed millions, of the wives at home hearing of their husbands' deaths and the people in the new country hearing that their families were wiped out. She nodded. This, she understood.

The leader looked at the bay before she continued.

"Rashat was young but he was the strongest shaman we had ever seen. When we first saw the god, we sent for him but he was already coming to us. While he trained, he had lived alone with his teacher, although he still issued edicts. He called for every shaman, and he and his teacher consulted the runes and the portents.

"They decided to stand against the god. My grandparents said they were frightened but they were also sure. They had done all their god asked and still, they were being slaughtered. As you said, it was not…just." Her smile was bitter. "They believed they were right to stand against it."

"And?" Dahti asked quietly.

"Maybe they were," the warrior said with a shrug. "But right and powerful are two different things. Rashat's mentor was struck down before his eyes—young for a shaman, not even fifty. He stood against the creature alone then, and he called the scriptures to it. The beast did not care.

"It struck at the villagers and he summoned the power of a storm to drive it away, but it flew back to lash at him again. He summoned a wave as high as this cliff to strike it into the deeps and lift rocks to shred its body…"

"It wasn't defeated, though," she said.

"No. It wasn't. Rashat was almost killed by that effort. The god feasted on our people while he lay as one dead. Eventually, some of the warriors were able to beat it back enough that it left —or perhaps it had simply eaten its fill. It disappeared into the sea and it has not come back, but we know it still lives."

"And Rashat?" Dahti asked.

"He lay alone for two full cycles of the moon. They say he ate nothing and drank nothing. One by one, the messengers returned to say the other tribes were dead as well and they had found their families gone and their homes destroyed." The warrior looked at her clasped hands. "There was no one else left to lead us, and so we begged Rashat to pick himself up and tell us what to do next. He…didn't."

"He is still…" Dahti could not find the word. "A recluse?"

"No." The leader sighed heavily. "He does everything asked of him. He fishes, he mends nets, he collects freshwater and prepares food. He will do anything at all, and do it well—save use his magic or train an apprentice. We have asked him to do so many times, and he always says the same thing—that the magic of the water tribe failed us and that he will let it pass from memory and die with him." She looked frankly at her. "And so we understand, truly, what it is to face your god. We would help you if we could. But Rashat will not help you and no one else knows how."

Dahti looked out at the sea. Now that she was in this water-rich place, she thought she could feel the tug of the magic. She told herself it was all in her head, but she didn't think it was. Her logic suggested that this was how Prima had made this place— full of magic and full of secrets waiting to be learned.

The AI had seen how much she liked magic and…had she made this place *for* her? She blinked rapidly and told herself that the faint stinging in her eyes was from the salt wind.

Finally, she asked, "Could I speak to him? Would you allow it?"

The leader looked nervous. "I will bring you to the village

elders. They can decide. I would say…do not try. Go, find someone else. Go to the earth tribes and seek out the air tribes. Rashat was once feared, and…well, it's easy to see why if you ever look into his eyes. There's something dark there. I would never, ever want to make him angry." She shuddered, then added defensively, "And if you think I'm a coward, ask anybody. They'll say the same."

"I don't doubt you," Dahti said thoughtfully. "Still, I too have seen the death of many I hold dear—and I have seen many people step forward to become the leader no one thought they could be. I would like to speak to your elders."

The warrior sighed quietly. "I warned you," she said glumly. "Well, come on. We might as well start now. I can't wait to see what they'll make of *this*."

CHAPTER ELEVEN

The walk to the village was beautiful, although if anything could make Dahti miss the dry heat of the plains, it was the humid heat of a jungle. Thankfully, the breeze off the water kept most of it to a bearable level.

"So you watch the tunnel, then," she called to the leader of the group, who had introduced herself as Atra.

"Nah," Atra responded and threw a grin over one shoulder. "No one's come looking for us in years—not from the other tribes, anyway. We go up there to watch the sea. Sometimes, humans like to bring their ships in and drop anchor and we don't want a fight. You were whistling, so we heard you in the tunnel. We were about as surprised as you were."

She smiled and acknowledged that she had begun to like these warriors. All were young and seemed to share Atra's belief in their tribe. They might not know their future or whether it would look anything like the past their grandparents knew, but they were determined to protect their people. She appreciated that in young people.

Traditions and norms changed. What never changed was that you should protect those close to you.

At the bottom of the hill, when they were engulfed in greenery, the team started along what could not even charitably be called a path. They must have known it by habit and sheer familiarity because they all followed the same sequence of steps without even looking at one another. There were no trail markers and no downtrodden areas she could see to provide clues.

What struck her most about the village was the silence. People didn't speak to one another or sing and so, when the group stepped into the perimeter of the settlement, it was a shock. People were present and they were working, but they were silent.

Her presence, at least, caused a noticeable stir. The warm green-brown of her skin was visibly different from that of the young soldiers around her. They now, under the gazes of their families and elders, looked like they wondered if they'd made the correct choice in bringing her with them.

Courage, she wanted to whisper to the group leader but she sensed that this was a choice the younger woman needed to make on her own.

Atra raised her chin and pointed toward a large hut at the back of the camp. "This way. The elders aren't waiting but they'll see us going there and join us." Under her breath, she added, "Hopefully."

How badly had the elders of this tribe mistreated their young ones if this was how things were? Dahti followed and her blood began to boil.

Inside the large hut and beyond a scrap of tattered cloth lay a room that was, indeed, empty. A plain pole was fixed in the middle to hold the roof up, windows that would provide an outlook over the sea were covered by reed screens, and threadbare cushions rested on the floor.

There was no art. That was her first thought once her eyes adjusted to the gloom enough to see.

The elders arrived quickly. Perhaps they wanted the outsider gone as soon as possible. Whatever the case, the eight of them entered and an older woman with tusks like Atra's gave the warrior a hard stare.

Dahti's lip curled.

When the elders were all seated, they waited in silence. Atra stepped forward and bowed.

"Elders, I present to you Dahti of the earth tribes, by way of the fire lands. She seeks the help of our tribe. I will let her present her petition." She stepped aside and gestured to her.

She nodded to those assembled. "Elders of the water tribe, I offer the joy of many villages that you still live. You have long been thought to be dead. Huwat, shaman of Mountain's Shadow, sends his regards."

"And why does an earth orc come bearing the word of a fire shaman?" one of the elders asked.

Her heart sank. She already knew what their answer would be.

Still, she had to try. "Huwat's village has been attacked by their god, much like your tribes were attacked by yours," she said. "Since the news of that attack, they have searched for the meaning behind it and have begun to suspect that the gods are not what they claim to be. They do not want to offer themselves in sacrifice to false gods, but there is only one tribe that has ever slain a fire god and that is yours. I was sent to learn from your shaman." She paused. "From Rashat."

"Rashat practices no magic," one of them said simply. "Our tribe has not existed for two generations, earth orc. There is nothing for you to learn here."

"But..." She looked around at them in confusion. "You *do* exist. You're here. You survived."

"We are not a tribe any longer," one of them said. "We are husks. We have bodies. We are orcs...perhaps. But we have no shaman and without a shaman, we have no soul. We have no gods, we have no rites, and we have no hymns."

Dahti looked at the young ones, who stood now with their gazes fixed firmly on the ground.

The silent village and the bare huts spoke volumes. The water tribe had been the most devout among the orcs and now, they had nothing. They did not sing their songs, which had all been hymns. They did not paint. None of the young orcs had tattoos or necklaces.

She might have grieved if she were not so angry—and she was incandescently angry. "Do you mean to tell me," she said, "that you have spent forty years or more wallowing in misery and raised your children and their children to not sing and not delight in their culture because you have *cast it aside?*"

"We have none of those things to give them," one of the elders said. "Our songs were to false gods. Our tattoos were in service to a monster. We burned the statues and forgot the songs. There was no one to guide us forward. What were we to do?"

"Guide your damned selves," she snapped.

Everyone in the hut responded with a hastily indrawn breath.

"Oh, be real," Dahti said harshly. "You can't tell me no one here wanted to sing or make tattoos or artwork. You held them all back. You put your babies to bed without lullabies and told your children you had no stories for them. It should have been clear years ago that Rashat wouldn't guide you, but you didn't choose anyone else, did you?"

Some of the elders hissed through their teeth, and one of them stared accusingly at the young warriors. "Did you tell this outsider our secrets?"

"If you have no soul, you have no secrets," she said contemptuously. "You let one man's despair drag you all into oblivion."

"Without a shaman, we have no—"

"According to the ways you *abandoned*," she snapped. "If you abandoned the rest of it, then why not this part?"

They looked at one another and one woman stood to face her.

"How many years have you seen, earth orc?"

"Eighty-four," she said promptly. She folded her arms and met their stares. "I don't care what you think. It's true. I have four children. I have ten grandchildren. I have seven great-grandchildren. And I left them to help a tribe that is being hunted by a god and, so *help* me, you will let me slap some sense into Rashat."

The old woman stood back, her arms folded in a mirrored gesture, and studied her. "Well, *that* was spoken like a grandmother, and no mistake."

Quietly, Atra said, "I thought you said your village was wiped out."

Dahti looked at her. The thought of her children and their children in graves made her eyes water, and it wasn't acting to say, "Leaving graves is also difficult."

Atra nodded.

The older woman drew her attention again. "If you are so old, you will understand when I say that we did this to protect our young ones. The songs we sang and the statues we made called destruction down upon us. We are not wise in the ways of the gods, and even those who were fell into death and despair. We do not go to the water's edge now, save by night. We do not sing songs that would carry on the wind. We love our children as much as you, earth orc."

That, she understood and she considered it before she responded.

"I honor your sacrifice, grandmother, but surely you know this is no answer."

"And yet, what other answer is there?" The woman looked her in the eyes. "A life with no songs still has joy. Perhaps we are no longer orcs. Perhaps we have no tribe. But we exist."

Dahti looked around, hoping something might present itself as an opportunity. They feared the return of the dragon, that much was clear. Everything they did was in fear of that. Where before, they had considered it a bargain that was harsh but fair and difficult but predictable, they now feared the impossibly high toll of it.

She had an idea of the one thing that might—*might*—jolt Rashat out of his despair.

It was a long shot. After forty years, he had grown accustomed to it and might never emerge from it.

Whatever the outcome, she had to try, though.

"This is no life," she said to them. "Not for you and not for *anyone*. Your god turned on you and I believe it was only the first one. Now, the fire tribe is menaced, and for all we know, the air tribe faces their god even as we speak or has been laid low like you. The orcs will never be able to live in peace or happiness until the false gods are brought low."

They stared at her with a terrible hunger in their eyes.

"I thought on it as I walked," Dahti said. "A water shaman was the only one ever to defeat a fire god. What if a fire shaman could have done the same for you? We will be stronger as *one people*. When those who call themselves gods—who do *not* bring the beasts or the rains—are gone, we can build cities and sing whatever songs we wish. But we cannot do it as separate tribes. We must restart the festivals. And first, we must band together to destroy those who would threaten our children."

One of the old men had a tear tracing down his cheek. His eyes were closed, his old face lined with pain.

"Let me speak to Rashat," she said urgently. "*Please.* He *must* understand what is at stake. It was not his failure and it is not only his people who will suffer if he allows this tradition to die."

The old woman smiled. "If you seek to train as a shaman, it is not our place to stop you. You never needed our permission."

"Don't you pull out old-fashioned sensibilities." Dahti stabbed a finger at her. "You made this as difficult as humanly possible. Orcably? As difficult as possible. I've spent considerable time around humans," she added when they stared at her. She looked at Atra. "Can you take me to Rashat?"

The woman seemed amused. "Yes. This way." She ducked out the door without waiting for the approval of the elders and held the cloth aside for her. As she led the way across the rough ground, she said in an undertone, "Thank you. I've heard so many times why we cannot sing or dance but never have I heard someone say the things I wanted to say in return." She looked quizzically at her. "Are you *sure* you're eighty-four?"

"Unfortunately, yes."

Atra smiled and gestured to a small hut nearby. "There. That is his hut. I—Rashat." She broke off and held a hand up. "Hello."

"Hello, Atra." He was tall and in his youth, he must have been very handsome. A tattoo had been started on one side of his torso but never finished. His white hair was cut short close to his head, and he kept his beard to a small layer of stubble. A hole in one of his heavy tusks suggested that an ornament had once been strung there.

He looked at Dahti and although his expression was mild, she understood what Atra meant about not wanting to make him angry. His black eyes were a void. In them, she saw years of self-hatred and despair, all combining into a terrible fury she was sure might spill out at any time.

Well, she wouldn't get anywhere by trying to avoid the issue. She planted her staff in the dirt and inclined her head.

"Rashat, I am Dahti of…Hunt. I come at the behest of Huwat of Mountain's Shadow. Their god hunts them, and only one tribe has ever defeated a fire god. You are the last heir of that tradition. I seek your knowledge."

Rashat stared at her. She was aware that, all around the village, people had stopped to watch this exchange.

He moved closer. At her side, Atra did not step back although she was rigid with fear. His nostrils flared and his big hands clenched.

"My line," he said, "has no power over gods. It is useless and it will pass out of memory with me. It gives nothing to this tribe."

"Once," Dahti told him, "all the tribes gathered each year and the traditions were used to strengthen one another—"

"*My line*," Rashat bellowed at her, "*has no power over gods. It will pass out of memory with me!*"

He stormed into the woods, leaving the warrior trembling at her side.

"I'm sorry," she told Dahti. "I'm so sorry. I thought maybe he would listen to you."

"Oh, Atra," she said and smiled. "This is *not* over yet."

CHAPTER TWELVE

Most of the villagers had either been very young or not yet born when the water dragon attacked. They were unfamiliar with the world Rashat had inhabited—the world he believed he was the heir to.

Still, they knew him.

Dahti started with Atra and one simple request: "Tell me your first memory of Rashat."

The warrior blew her breath out and her gaze focused on the middle distance. Then, her face cleared and she looked both embarrassed and worried. "Oh, I know what it was. I always try not to remember this."

She waited but didn't look at the woman. Life had taught her that if you rushed in too soon, people would draw away.

"I was very little," Atra said. "But old enough to know right from wrong—well, what my parents wanted me to do or not do, you know. I knew they didn't want me to be loud when I played and I knew that none of us were supposed to talk to Rashat. Or about him."

"Not even about him?" she asked before she could stop herself.

"I asked why he didn't have children or grandchildren," the woman explained. "They made all kinds of weird faces and told me not to ask questions about Rashat and *never* to speak to him. Well, what can you say to make a child insatiably curious? That."

Dahti, who keenly remembered her failures in this area—as well as watching her children fail the same way—couldn't suppress a laugh.

"So, I waited until they were doing chores…" Atra leaned her forehead on one palm. She blushed, although on a water orc, it was a deep blue color. "And I marched *right* up to him and asked why he didn't have a wife and children and why everyone always said his name all funny."

"Oh." She clapped a hand over her mouth. "Oh, dear. Oh, dear."

"You know that look of absolute horror adults have when you do that kind of thing?" the warrior asked. "I still remember that look. Not from him, of course. He knelt, all normal—oh, I hate remembering this. I should have simply listened to them."

She smiled, patted the girl on the shoulder, and wished she would hurry up with the story.

"He said he had no wife and child because he did not deserve them," Atra said. "And he spoke so normally, too. He told me that when he was younger, he was supposed to protect the tribe and he had failed, that he should have been killed but he lived as a reminder to all of us."

"A reminder of what?"

"I never got to find out." She hunched her shoulders. "My mother came and hauled me across the village and up the path there to where we found you, yes? And she said if I couldn't follow the rules, I could go live with the fire tribes and bring *their* gods down on *their* heads, but she wouldn't keep me here to kill everyone."

Dahti, who rather thought parents went too easy on children nowadays, was shocked to hear a story of parenting much harsher than what she had experienced. She stared at Atra, and finally managed a strangled, "My goodness."

The warrior shrugged. "She was right."

"To tell a child to leave home if she can't follow rules—why, Atra, every child breaks rules."

Atra considered this. "I think it's different for us," she said finally. "I think many things are different for us. You were so angry about the songs and the art, but that's simply the way we've lived. If we attract the attention of the god, who knows how many could die? Who knows if we'll even survive it?"

She opened her mouth to ask what the point was of surviving as a tribe if there were no traditions passed down and if every breath was taken in the shadow of fear. Caution stepped in, however, and she did not give voice to the words. These people still lived and they wanted to keep living.

That was enough for her. She gave one pained thought to the fire tribe, who even now fled through the plains, and prayed that she could convince Rashat to help her with enough time to spare.

"Thank you," she said gravely and she went to ask someone else.

This time, she aimed older and eventually went to help a man with the traps he was laying in the stream. She could see the gray peppered through his hair, which was a good sign.

He gave her an alarmed look when she appeared, but she was a competent hand at snares and traps and once he saw that she could fix the ties and set the traps, he relaxed.

They worked in silence until he said finally, "You can't have come all this way merely to be one of our tribe."

"No?" She smiled. "I have no tribe of my own, you know. Plague took them months ago. Why should I not settle here?"

He looked at her and snorted. "Everyone knows what you said to the elders."

"For a village where no one speaks much," she said, "it's amazing how fast word travels."

"Simply because we don't talk loudly doesn't mean we don't talk." He stood and shook his hands. "That's all of these. Come along if you're going to help."

Dahti followed him, still silent and watchful, until he turned to look over his shoulder at her.

"What?" she asked innocently.

"Well? Are you going to ask? And don't say, 'ask what.' Ask whatever you came here to ask." He shrugged. "Not that I don't appreciate the help with the traps, mind."

"You don't fish in the ocean anymore, then." Dahti watched him closely.

"Sometimes." He shook his head. "It's tempting. But every visit there tempts the god to return and finish what he started."

"Why not leave?" she asked him curiously. "You could go to the plains or…the mountains."

He inclined his head at her. "Do you not feel it?"

"Feel what?" She looked around nervously, half-afraid she had a giant spider on her back or something.

"The call of your ancestral lands." He frowned at her. "The sea is a part of us. It might be home to the god who wants us dead but if we were to leave it, that would be the death of us. We would no longer be water orcs."

Dahti suppressed her small sound of satisfaction. That was the key—or, if not the only one, at least one of them. With no larger tribe and no shamans, the one link these orcs had to their past was the sea that was both their soul and their deepest terror.

"I wonder what it's like," she said softly. The sea was all around them and it permeated everything. "To have it be such a part of you and not be able to touch it."

The orc looked at her. "Yes," he said at last. "I never knew the sea as they did—I was born the year after and it has always been the source of our terror. Still, I feel it in my bones, every tide and every wave. I cannot imagine life without the sound and smell of it. And it's worse, you know—for *him*."

She looked sharply at him.

"The children know him as…an uncle, perhaps. One you don't want to make mad but a person like any other. When I was a child, you could feel him coming from across the village. His pain was like the sharpest spear and always pointed toward the sea."

It took Dahti longer than it should have to understand. "You were born with magic," she said quietly. "You would have been his apprentice."

His head jerked up and he stared at her.

She realized he hadn't known.

Afraid to lose his willingness to speak, she gestured to the stream behind them. "You've always been better at setting traps than anyone else, haven't you? Better at finding fresh water. And you can feel the waves…and Rashat's pain. You know how much it hurt him to give it up."

"No," the man said shortly. "I don't. Whatever talent I have—might have had—his is far greater. They said he was five when he held the tides back one day."

Dahti knew her eyes must be as round as dinner plates.

"He was beyond anyone else," the orc told her. "None of the shamans could match him. My parents said to me, 'you have only ever known him as a broken man but once, he was whole.'" He thought for a moment before he added, "Perhaps they do not say it in your tribe, but in ours, we say a person is only whole when their being and their purpose are aligned. None of us have been whole since the god came but few were ever as whole as Rashat. To have that and then lose it?" He shook his head. "It is not a fate I would wish on anyone."

She returned to the traps. There simply were no words to respond to this, only a hollow feeling in her chest and one she remembered all too well.

It was what she had felt in the months after Harry died.

The comparison was the closest she could find but it wasn't the same. Harry had lived a full life and they'd had time together before he died. It was nowhere near as tragic as losing her family, her home, her spouse, and her life's purpose in one fell swoop at twenty.

Still, it had felt as if a piece of her was not so much dead as cut away—gone and unreachable. The thought of such a pain magnified was almost more than she could bear.

After a time, a cleared throat made her look up as the man backed away to make room for Atra's grandmother. The old woman took his place without a word and began to work on the nets and traps.

"What do you hope for?" she asked finally.

"I never made a secret of it," Dahti said. There wasn't much inflection in her voice. What she needed from them—from Rashat—was too much to ask.

She saw that now.

"What you want is for Rashat to be whole again," the woman said. "But you don't see—he was never whole."

Dahti frowned at her. "That man said—"

"Jemad never knew him," Atra's grandmother interrupted. "I did. And I can tell you, girl, he was never whole. He had a purpose, true enough, but he never had a self. How could he? From the time he was a baby, he had the hopes of the tribe on his shoulders. He knew what they expected of him before he knew his name. Small wonder he thought to kill a god."

"Are you saying he wanted to kill a god *before* the god came?" she asked.

"That's what I'm saying." The woman tied a knot deftly, her old fingers still nimble. "How else to set his destiny? That's one thing we all need. He couldn't back away from it, oh, no. He breathed magic and always had. The one chance he had to do something all his own was to be *more* than they expected."

"How do you know this?" she asked her softly. She remembered all too well the way she'd assessed people in her youth—

people she'd never known. Who was to say if this old woman was right?

"We saw," the woman said simply. "Everyone wanted to be him. All our parents wished it was their child with the talent—except he was taken away to study with the shamans and his parents were alone. He was never theirs and was always the tribe's. We still envied him, but…I think we all knew it was easier to have our little dalliances and our feasts than it was to live in a hut and study magic with the shamans."

Dahti nodded.

"I heard whispers," the woman told her. "They were horrified at what he said. But he'd read the histories and he knew there was a time when things had been different. He said we were chaining ourselves by bowing to it. The rest of us kids liked to side with him—we thought we were so daring." She paused, her head bowed. "When the god came, I think we all thought he could defeat it. He wasn't the only one."

She paused and looked from the old woman to the village.

One question remained. "And no one could persuade him to…be a shaman again? To heal himself?"

"Child." The woman looked at her. "He thinks all of this is his fault. He thinks he called the god down on us. We did what we could—we took the knives from him and the saltwater he tried to drink. We convinced him to take food. We thought it was a kindness to help him survive." She looked over her shoulder. "I am not certain it was. All I ask is if you try to make him a shaman once more, keep in mind what we did not—what you ask him to do. If he does it, he will live with the consequences of it for years. Was it truly a mercy to give him decades of life tainted with the knowledge that his failure let his village die drowning? I am not certain."

Dahti felt cold, then hot. She nodded and finished one more knot.

"Thank you, grandmother." It was almost funny the way such

words came to her in this young body. She was almost certainly older than her.

The woman said nothing as Dahti walked away.

Now that she had heard them speak of Rashat, she could see something more clearly. His hut was not on the worst patch of land as she had immediately assumed. She thought it was a self-imposed penalty that he had built it on bare rock, ever-wet with the flow of the river.

He needed that to survive, though. His magic was part of who he was and the touch of the water kept him sane.

She knew he was inside from the way the others watched and whispered while she approached.

It took effort but she ignored them. At the water's edge, she knelt and focused on it—the trickle of it and the way it was a caress and a threat all in one. Then, she stood and readied her powers.

Part of the problem was that she didn't know how to use water. The first spell came out as an earth-shock, a clod of mud that thudded into the water and bobbed away on the stream before it broke into pieces.

"Hmph." Dahti grunted.

It wasn't wasted effort, however, and she thought she could feel his interest from inside the hut. She sat in the shallow part of the stream and began to make magic of all kinds—rock spurs, clouds of dust, and clods of mud. She almost managed a mist of water droplets once but otherwise, she didn't come close.

Which was why she wasn't surprised when heavy footsteps sounded behind her and Rashat said, both furious and pained, "What in the twelve hells do you think you're doing?"

CHAPTER THIRTEEN

"Do you think it's working?" Tina asked.

"It's hard to say from here." Justin pillowed his chin on his hands and watched the distant figures in the village.

Beyond a very cryptic few sentences, they hadn't been able to get much out of Prima. In fact, the AI claimed it had no idea what Dahti was up to. Now, it chimed in with, *"It's hard to say from inside the game too."*

The young woman snickered.

"Is something funny to you?" Prima asked dangerously.

"Yeah. You get suuuuuper freaking huffy when you don't understand human behavior." She looked at the sky with a grin.

"May I remind you that I am the one holding these rocks up?"

"Oh, come on." She rolled onto her back to hold the conversation.

"You know I'm not where you're looking any more or less than I was where you were looking in the first place."

"I like to focus somewhere while I'm talking," Tina said with great dignity. "I don't suppose you'd make yourself an avatar."

"And be closed into a tiny prison with limited senses, speed, and strength? No. The mere thought is terrifying."

"Hey!" She sat up. "It's not that bad. Stop making it sound like a terrible thing."

"You might want to be a little quieter," Justin said nervously. He patted her arm. "The wind keeps shifting and if they hear us… well, I don't trust them to not shoot."

"She's being rude," Tina said as if it were self-explanatory.

"Yes, I know, but *again*, I would prefer to not get shot."

"You are such a pansy."

"Isn't he?" the woman agreed.

"Hey! Ugh." He shook his head. "I knew I shouldn't give you two a common enemy. You're both insane."

"Well, that's rude." Prima gave a little huff. *"And you shouldn't take it as an insult, Tina. It isn't as difficult for you to be in that body."*

Tina sighed. "I suppose being born in a body is very different from existing as a—"

"After all, you don't have the cognitive capabilities for it to be limiting."

"Hey!"

"Ooookay, we will one hundred percent be shot." Justin ushered her off the rock. "Prima, as amusing as you would find it if we *were* shot, do you think you could find it in your heart to get us out of here and back to Insea?"

"Thank you for acknowledging my sacrifice in this matter," the AI said graciously. *"They are making preparations to take you two out of the game, so I will do that directly. One moment."*

The world melted around them and he opened his eyes. The pod lid was already open and bright lights shined on him. He expected to need to squint but as far as his optic nerves knew, he'd recently been outside in bright sunlight and this wasn't very different from that.

He accepted Nick's hand to sit.

"You were being *so* rude," Tina's voice said nearby.

Justin rolled his eyes. "I don't think I—"

"Not *you*," Tina said. "These guys." She glared at Amber and the others. "Which one of you runs Prima?"

For a moment, all three of them looked panicked before they plastered identical, too-big smiles in place.

"Um…" Amber grimaced.

"It's a group effort," Jacob said.

"Yeah," Nick finished.

Tina looked at them. She looked at Justin and focused on the team again. "Um. Okay."

"Right," Jacob said.

"Yeah," Nick added.

"We need to get you to your interview!" Amber said to Justin as if this were the most exciting thing that had ever happened.

"*Yeah*," Nick said. Jacob gave him a sharp look and he shut up.

"That was weird," Justin muttered to Tina as they left.

She frowned and shrugged. "I think so too, but then again, they're always weird."

"You're thinking of DuBois."

"No. I'm thinking of all of them." She gave him a cheeky grin. "It's why we fit in so well here."

They walked to the interview suite hand in hand. After his time in the game today, he felt energetic and happy. Still, he began to feel winded when he arrived at the interview and felt a spike of panic at the sight of the reporters.

To his surprise, Anna Price waited outside the door, as elegant as usual. Justin wondered if her shirts ever wrinkled or if she had sacrificed something to the devil to avoid that. She looked impossibly well put-together.

Or maybe it was simply that the piercing stare made him forget everything else because whenever Anna Price looked at him, he wanted to flee in the opposite direction, screaming at an unmanly pitch. The woman ran a company that partnered with several black ops wings of the US Military, and you could tell that when you looked at her.

Right now, she was smiling. He decided that could mean everything.

"I hope your visit to New York has been good thus far," she said to them and made sure to share her terrifying attention with Tina as well. "Mr. Williams, if I could have a moment of your time before you go in?"

"Yes?" Justin said, hoping his voice hadn't broken too audibly.

"Excellent. May I speak in front of Ms. Castro?"

He nodded. Tina, meanwhile, looked terrified that Price remembered who she was.

"The reporters have been informed that no audio or video is to be taken in the room and they will be able to check quotes provided by us. The PIVOT team tells me that you've been briefed on the few items that are not to be discussed due to privacy concerns but otherwise, I want to be clear that you are allowed to share whatever you feel comfortable sharing. You are also free to not answer any questions as you see fit."

"Er..." He wanted this to be over so he wasn't under her dragon-stare anymore, but he also wasn't sure what she meant. "Like, if I think they're looking for info they shouldn't have?"

Price smiled almost gently.

Almost.

"The crash and your recovery may be a very emotional topic," she said. "If you feel uncomfortable or do not want to continue the interview, there will be no repercussions."

Justin, who had not considered any of this, looked at Tina.

"We are glad of your help with publicity," Price told him. "I simply wanted to speak to you before you went in to make sure you didn't feel pressured. Have a good rest of your day, both of you, and perhaps I'll see you again before you leave."

She strode away and he stared at her back.

"Does she frighten you as much as she frightens me?" Tina asked. Her lips barely moved as if she was afraid the woman would turn and see them.

"Her tone and her words are both so nice, but I still feel like I'm being threatened," he muttered, following her example.

"Cheer up," she said finally. "If they wanted to turn you into a lab rat, they already had their chance."

"Lab rat?"

"You know—dark, spooky experiments. Tracking chips." She waggled her eyebrows. "Controlling your thoughts."

"What if they already did that?"

"Then there's nothing to be done about it, is there?"

"Have I mentioned how nice it is to have you here as a supportive girlfriend in this trying time?" Justin looked at her and his mouth twitched.

"Isn't it?" Tina said serenely. "Come on, let's go in."

The interview, after all the build-up, wasn't as frightening as Justin or Anna Price had worried it would be. With Tina seated nearby and the ever-present whirr of the Diatek audio recorders, the reporters were very respectful.

"Mr. Williams," one of them said. "In earlier interviews, you and your parents alluded to the fact that you had some communication. What can you tell us about the first time you heard from them?"

"Oh." He thought back on what now seemed worlds away. "That was a lot to digest because I wasn't yet aware of why I was in the game."

"You were aware that it was a game, though."

"Yeah, it was very clear. Like, I had game stats and an interface and all that, and I died in the game almost right off the bat and then came back, so it wasn't like I thought I'd woken up in the wilderness to fight wolves with a rusty sword."

That drew a few chuckles.

"I thought I must have started a new VR game on my headset," he said. "I wasn't thinking very clearly at the time, of course. You find yourself in a game and your mind simply fills the blanks. I kept thinking I should stop and leave it and then didn't do it, and

I think they worried that I might panic if I couldn't take the headset off as I expected to. So they sent me a letter." He caught sight of Tina's face. "What?"

"I've never heard this story," she explained.

"Oh." He took her hand. "Um—where was I? Oh. So, my parents filmed a video for me and so did Dr. DuBois, telling me what was going on and all that. They also told me I had to be careful to not die in the game because it could stop my heart and I wasn't in very good shape." To his horror, he felt his throat thicken. "It…was a lot to take in."

Tina squeezed his hand.

"I can't imagine," the reporter said. As far as Justin could tell, he was completely sincere. "Being in a near-death state is very frightening and as far as we know, you're the first person ever to know for certain that you were in a coma. What can you tell people out there who might be thinking of writing to PIVOT on behalf of family members who are comatose?"

"Uh…" He chewed his lip. "Could I think for a moment? Um… Okay. Well, I think a big thing is that the game is different for everyone. I'm good at video games—I mean, I've played them forever. But right now, there are people in the game who haven't ever played before. For them, it's a completely different experience.

"I guess the biggest thing is that people will have friends around them—the game is so good at bringing characters to life. But at the same time, they'll be alone. You have to trust them to get themselves to where they need to be to wake up."

People nodded.

"Now we know you can't tell us about other people in the game, but what do you think of when you imagine the future of this treatment?" another reporter asked. "Are there any places you think it could be useful?"

"I'm not sure," Justin said. "It's merely so powerful in terms of being immersive. I tried to pick something up the other day and it was funny because I swung it like a sword—like I would have in the game. I knew the motion, but my muscles aren't as strong here as they were there so it feels strange to be back in the real world sometimes."

The interview continued with his most amusing moment in-game—"definitely my mother screaming hysterically and using a ridiculously large spell to kill a spider"—and his most difficult one. He told them about leveling up skills like Clumsy but he steered clear of mentioning Prima.

He wasn't quite sure why, though.

At length, he and Tina waved goodbye and headed out. In the hallway, Jacob gave them a quick thumbs-up.

"You did great," he said. "Because the treatment is in testing, they'll run the articles by us before publishing, but I think it's safe to say they loved you. Go get some rest and we can get you in here for more game time if you want before you go."

"Awesome." He followed him to the elevator and leaned against the wall.

"Another room service night?" Tina asked.

"Would you mind? I know it's stupid to be here of all places and not try the food."

"So we'll come back sometime," she said. "What use is a schmancy meal if you're miserable?"

"That's a very good point," Jacob interjected. "Not to…eavesdrop." As the elevator doors slid open, he plastered a smile on, waved, then turned and said to Justin, "Pray for me."

"Why, who's here?" He looked out to where a woman in her fifties or sixties was waiting. She was dressed simply in colored jeans and a sweater.

"It's one of Dotty's daughters," Jacob said in an undertone. "She wasn't a huge fan of her mother going into the game."

"Do you want me to talk to her?" he asked.

"Would you? That would be amazing." He led them through security. "Ellen, hi. This is Justin Williams."

"I've seen some of your interviews." The woman looked intrigued. "I would love to talk more sometime. Right now, I have to go see my mom. I promised I would spend some time in the game with her."

"You can also see her playing," Jacob said.

"And I'd be happy to talk to you," Justin said. "I'm sure Jacob can pass my information on."

"Well, thank you. It means a lot." Ellen looked like she was forcing things but finally said, "The team is doing great work and my mother is…very happy here. I'm grateful."

She went to security and pulled her ID out, and Jacob muttered, "Well, I'll be damned. Maybe she's not planning to shiv me."

"Good luck," Justin said. "We'll go get some ridiculously over-priced burgers."

"It's the only way to get them in New York," the other man said with a shrug.

"What in the twelve hells do you think you're doing?" Rashat demanded.

Dahti looked at him with real interest. "You have *twelve*?"

He drew breath to launch into a tirade but at this response, he paused uncertainly and stared at her. It proved to be only a momentary lapse, but she enjoyed it nonetheless.

"Do you think *you'll* be the one to kill the water god?" His nostrils flared.

She resisted a smile. "What are they all for?"

"What?"

"You have twelve hells. What are all of them for? We have seven, one for each of the seven deadly sins. Do you have twelve deadly sins? Oooh, what did you add? Let me guess." She was having fun with this. "Um...talking at the movies. Obviously. Inviting someone over for dinner and only serving salad."

"Earth orc—"

"Spoiling the endings of books," she said. "Okay, we're up to... ten. Two more."

"*Get out of this stream!*" Rashat bellowed.

The village went very silent. Several people had stopped in

mid-stride and hunched their shoulders as if hoping to not be seen. When he looked at them, several gasped audibly before everyone scattered.

Dahti sighed and stood. Her pants were sopping wet and cold but she wouldn't let that ruin this for her. She folded her arms and stared calmly at him. She wanted him to admit a truth to her that he'd never admitted to anyone, let alone himself. If she wanted him to do *that*, she needed to get him hopping mad first.

"You have all of *them* trained good," she said. Her tone wasn't particularly respectful.

Rashat gaped for a minute before his brows snapped together in a fearsome scowl. She knew how this would go. He would build up slowly.

She didn't give him the chance, though, and looked around the village. "I suppose it's a real good setup you have here," she continued and gave him a mocking grin. "A whole village who thinks about *nothing* except how to keep you from getting mad. They even tell all their kids about it, don't they? 'Don't bother Rashat.' 'Don't make Rashat mad.'" She injected a sing-song quality into her tone.

He took a single step toward her. His face was dangerous now. "You should think very carefully before—"

"Oh, *please.* I've lived eighty-four years on this earth. Do you think I've never seen this playbook before? You take one step, you narrow your eyes a little, you keep your voice steady but you make it dangerously quiet, and you point—yep, that finger right there. You say something threatening but you don't spell it out and you let your target fill in all the blanks." She rolled her eyes. "You're so lazy. You can't even threaten people on your own."

"I'm *lazy*?" He was almost too blindsided to be angry.

"Lazy is your middle name, boy," Dahti retorted. "You've coasted for your whole damned life. You didn't have to do all the chores when you were little because you were the *special one*. You were going to be a *shaman*, so while everyone else hauled water and cleaned clothes, you could merely sit in a little hut and think about the universe."

"That is *not* what shaman training is like—"

"Then you encountered a little bad luck and you found someone you couldn't beat, and what did you do? Oh, *right.*" Dahti was getting into the swing of this now. "You stopped doing even your work as a shaman anymore. You made them run around, waiting on you hand and foot, trying to coax a single bite of food into you at a time—while they were trying to *rebuild their damned lives and bury their dead.* You didn't care about *that*, oh, no. *You* needed everyone to focus on you. 'Poor Rashat, he couldn't stand up to the God.'"

Rashat's chest heaved now and a vein throbbed at his temple. She had no doubt that this was working.

"And now I hear you're a model citizen!" she told him brightly. "You help with the fishing. You even carry water now." She clapped her hands. "I've never heard of anyone so devoted to their tribe. Do you want a medal? Or a statue, maybe? Or maybe we should write hymns about you! After all, how *do* we deal with such a *paragon* walking amongst us?"

"Shut up!" Rashat bellowed. "Shut up! Shut! Up!"

"Or what?" Dahti asked him mockingly. "You'll *glower* at me again?"

"I'll throw you out of this village with my own two hands!" He snarled at her in rage.

"Well, that would make an interesting change—you doing your own work for a change."

He snatched a stave up from the ground. Ready to keep fish traps in place, it was sharpened at one end. He jabbed it at her and she could see the amount of raw power still left in his body.

She could also tell he had never been trained with weapons.

"I will send you back to your tribe in pieces," he said from between gritted teeth, "before I let you endanger these people."

"Oh, is that *your* job?" She ducked an unsteady thrust of the spear with ease. "You'll have to do better than that."

"Get out!" Rashat yelled at her. "Leave this place and never return, and so help me, if you've called the god back to this village, I'll—"

"What, fail again? Make everyone soothe *you* again instead of mourning their own families?" she shouted in response. "Tell another generation of kids how you failed and how they should feel so sorry for you while they live without a shaman, without the sea, and without safety? What use *are* you?"

"*I am nothing but a warning!*" His face contorted and he lunged at her like a madman, raining blows and jabs. Although he'd never been trained, he was still strong and he was angry. "I am a joke from the gods. I was made to be a laughingstock!"

"You were given power beyond measure!" Dahti snatched a stave as well and struck his aside. Pain burst through her hands and forearms at the jolt of impact, but she turned her thoughts away. She needed every scrap of focus for the dual purposes of goading him and staying alive.

Man, he was pissed off.

"Of all the self-indulgent *crap!*" she shouted disdainfully. His stave thrust toward her and she only barely made it out of the way in time. She resisted the urge to punch him in the nose while his arms were overextended and instead, danced away. "You know the truth."

"Oh? What *truth* is that? Since you apparently know everything." He bared his teeth at her and growled.

"What came here was never a god," she told him contemptuously. "You wanted it to be a god so you could be chosen by one. You wanted it to be a god so you could defeat one, but you knew the whole time that you getting this power was nothing more than random *chance*. And you knew that 'god' was nothing more than an overgrown dragonfly who wanted its prey to line up neatly and traipse into its mouth!"

Rashat's next blow—thankfully a swing of the stave instead of a thrust—caught her on the side of the ribs and she hissed in pain. He hadn't managed to crack any bones, thank goodness, but it had been far from comfortable.

"You *knew*," Dahti yelled at him, "that you would *never* kill it! Water magic against a water dragon? You needed fire, you needed air, or you needed earth. You must have realized it when you fought."

At a distant roll of thunder, she looked up to see storm clouds gathering. They didn't scud across the sky but instead, swirled above the village.

They said he could make storms, Atra had said.

He did magic as naturally as he breathed, her grandmother remembered.

Good. She adjusted her grasp around the stave and settled into a fighting stance, her gaze locked on Rashat's.

"Say it," she told him.

"Say *what*?"

"Say. It. The truth." She felt the first patter of rain on her skin. "Say what you think of these people."

"I *hate* them!" He screamed at her and the rain burst with the loudest crack of thunder she'd ever heard. "I wish every one of them had died and I wish I had too!"

Ellen followed Jacob through the hallways of the Diatek building. Everything still seemed vaguely familiar after the party the other day.

"So..." She tried to come up with something to say. "Um. What's it like to go into the game for the first time?"

The look he gave her seemed a little wary, but he answered readily enough. "It's kind of jarring for the very first time. Disconcerting is probably a better word for it, I guess. Your brain has only ever received sensory data from your body, so it knows how to interpret what we send—it's all merely electrical signals, after all—but it's confusing to have it come from somewhere else."

"Ah," she said, not quite sure she understood that.

"And some people have trouble moving in the game at first," he added. "It's a thing where they have to send muscle impulses the same way they normally do, but…well, have you ever sat at your keyboard and forgotten how to make your fingers type your password?"

Ellen snorted surprised laughter. "Yes, I have."

"Like that," Jacob said with a smile. "And then you start thinking about it, but the more you think—"

"The worse it gets!" she finished excitedly. "I thought I was the only one."

"Nope." He shook his head. "Nope, that's everyone." He pushed the door to the lab open. "So, we'll…what's going on?"

Everyone in the lab was clustered around one of the pods and some of the others beckoned to them urgently.

"You have to see this," one of them said.

"She is tearing him a *new* one," said another.

"Who?"

"The shaman in the village. Damn, I would *not* want this woman to get angry at me." They returned to what they were watching.

"Um," Jacob said. "So…I could get you prepped—"

"Are you kidding? They're talking about my mother, right?" Ellen gestured at the screen. "I *have* to see this. Her lectures were *legendary* when we were little."

Everyone whipped around at once to stare at her and eyes went wide. Then, as a unit, they parted to let her through. It occurred to her that they were somewhat scared of her mother— and by extension, of her. Curiously, she moved closer to watch.

And when she heard what was going on, she couldn't help but

burst out laughing. This was her mother, all right. She was giving this man the dressing down of his life.

Ellen had to say, though, she was glad her mother hadn't gone full tilt with *them.*

"Is that a *spear?*"

"Um…" Jacob said.

"Okay, move over. I *gotta* see this."

<hr>

The rain fell in sheets, but Rashat didn't seem to care in the least. He charged at Dahti with the scream of a man who had nothing left to live for.

He didn't, after all. She had her suspicions as to the only reason he was still alive.

Well, she would see. Hopefully, she was right.

She threw herself into the fight with a will and reflected that this would be so much easier if the staves glowed. They were too difficult to see in the darkness and the rain—except, of course, when lightning cracked across the sky.

"You didn't let them live without a shaman because of any noble purpose," she shouted, "you did it because you hated them!"

"I wanted to save them!" Rashat screamed at her. "I gave everything to that fight. I had nothing else but my talent. I *was* nothing else!"

Dahti said nothing. She ducked under a wild swing and scrabbled away awkwardly on the wet, rocky ground.

"All of them told me I was born to bring glory to the tribe." His voice was raw now. "I was nothing to them but my magic. None of them ever cared for me. I wanted to kill the gods so I could break the cycle and leave. So a child could be born with magic and be nothing more than a child to them. I wanted to tear the whole thing to the ground!"

Her stave struck home and thwacked against his knuckles,

and he dropped his with a cry of pain. Now, she went on the offensive and drove him back ruthlessly.

"You still cared," she called to him. "You say that, but you wanted them to be safe. You regretted letting them down."

"Of course I did!" The cry was despairing. "You didn't see the bodies. You didn't see the blood of your family running down that beast's jaws. It took everything from us!"

"So. Help. Me. Kill. It." Dahti punctuated each word with a shout and a strike. She threw one foot up and kicked him full in the chest into an ungainly sprawl. "For the love of all gods, Rashat. It's been long enough."

The rain stopped. As quickly as they'd come, the clouds began to fade. He stared at her from where he lay, broken and despairing.

"You carried a burden no one should carry," Dahti told him grimly. "I'll not deny it. If you asked them outright, none of them would deny it either. But right *now*, you have two generations of your tribe that never did a godsdamned thing to you and you've punished them for their ancestors' mistakes like a selfish fool." She walked closer to plant the stave on his chest and watched him flinch. "You were put on a pedestal and never allowed to be anything but a shaman until your powers weren't the thing that could save them. And then they *still* looked to you and you hated them for it, but can you blame them, Rashat? They saw their god in the flesh. They needed hope. They needed *something*."

His head dropped back onto the ground and his eyes squeezed shut.

"You've had forty years to wallow in this," she said, her voice hard. "No more. I don't care how selfish your reasons were for wanting the gods dead—they're false gods, and it was a good goal. So right now, *you'll* teach me water magic and *I'll* help you kill your god, and *together,* we will go back and begin killing every single dragon we can get our hands on until your people are free and they can start over. Do you understand me?"

He opened his eyes and stared at her.

"And then maybe the screams you hear will stop," she said softly. "Maybe then, you can give the lost their burial rites because you can tell them that they were avenged."

Rashat lay motionless and stared at the sky. The clouds continued to dissipate without his rage to sustain them.

She had done all she could so she waited, leaning on her stave.

Finally, he pushed up. She held a hand out but he did not take it. He stood and looked at her.

"Forty years," he said simply. He looked out at the sea and she saw the longing in him.

"You won't have to fear what you are any longer," she told him.

He looked sharply at her. "Do you think that's what I care about?"

"Yes." She smiled. "I think it's part of it. As it should be. Your powers should help your tribe, Rashat, but they're *yours*. Use them for yourself, too."

"I'm too old for that," he said and his voice was equal parts amused and sad.

"It's never too late." Dahti picked his stave up and handed it to him. "I'd use that as a walking stick, if I were you—unless, of course, you want to learn how to use it."

"I might," he said contemplatively. She sensed it was almost his kind of joke. "I'll have enough free time after the god is dead, after all." Now, he gave her a sharp-toothed, bloodthirsty grin. "We'll start training tomorrow at dawn. Be in the center of the town square and don't be late or I'll wake you how my mentor used to wake me. With a bucket of ice-cold ocean water."

She snickered and watched as he strode away, his chin up and his gaze sweeping the world. He moved beyond hearing and she heard the others begin to creep out of their huts.

"You did it," Atra said from behind her. She stood with the

others and all of them were wide-eyed. "What did you say to him?"

Better they didn't know for now. She smiled. "I told him forty years was long enough to wait for payback," she said. She looked at them. "And that god will get payback. He's about to find out that it's a bitch."

"Dahti," Prima said. *"You have a guest in the game. I'll make people think you and Rashat are both taking the day for meditation before you begin your training. If you go to the seashore and follow the signs, you'll find your guest."*

Dahti nodded and set off. She had to admit she was curious.

Quickly, she pushed through the forest. She had decided not to follow the stream because she wanted a better idea of the environment she was working in. The dwarven book about earth magic crept into her thoughts—how it could be the raw heat of magma or the delicacy of dust motes hanging in the air, and how it encompassed both weathered mountains and growing plants.

This forest was a place of water, of course, being near the shore, but it was also a place of earth and she could almost hear it singing.

"Prima?"

"Yes?"

"Please don't let me get bitten by anything poisonous."

The AI snickered. *"I wondered when you'd remember that tropical forests can be dangerous."*

"Mm-hmm." She spent a brief moment wishing she could

thwack Prima with a stick the same way she had done to Rashat. It was a vain hope and she knew it but it was also a very satisfying mental image.

The seashore wound around an outcropping of gray rock, and she followed a carefully-laid line of seashells that disappeared in her wake, swept away conveniently by the waves. It was beautiful there, with the warm water lapping at her feet. She would spend every moment wishing she were there if she lived nearby.

No doubt, the water tribe *did* wish it.

Dahti stopped when she came around the point. *"Ellen?"*

"What do you think?" Her daughter turned with a smile, then gave a little shriek of fright. "Good God, it's one thing to see it on a screen, but…you're *huge*." Her nose wrinkled. "And you smell," she added. "You smell so bad, Mom."

"I'm aware, thank you." She studied her daughter curiously. "So you decided to be a mage?"

"What? Oh, the robes?" Ellen looked at them. "No, I don't have any powers at all. They asked if I wanted anything 'cool' like leather armor." She rolled her eyes. "I said they'd clearly never seen a sixty-something woman in leather pants."

She responded with a shout of laughter. "And what did they say to that?"

"They fell over themselves trying to tell me it would be fine and I still looked so good for my age." Ellen laughed at the memory. "Ah, young people." She turned and looked at the sky. "It's a *paradise* here."

"Isn't it?" Dahti wandered to a bench that had appeared out of nowhere. "Thank you, Prima."

"You're welcome. Refreshments?"

"Please."

A table burst into being as well, loaded with dishes both familiar and strange, from shredded chicken and roast potatoes, to yellow rice studded with fruit and nuts, and loaves of bread. Two chilled glasses of lemonade sweated at one end. She took one to Ellen and sipped hers in appreciation. It was exactly the right combination of sweet and tart.

"Mmm," her daughter said. She settled onto the bench.

She saw the smile falter. "What is it?"

"It's, um…the smell."

"Right. Prima, I don't suppose you could do something about that for a few minutes?"

"*Of course,*" the AI said a touch too sweetly. "*I'm only running the entire world. I barely have a thing on my plate right now. It's embarrassing, honestly.*"

"Yeah, yeah." The smell vanished. "Thank you."

Prima muttered something indistinguishable.

Ellen took a sip of her lemonade and stole a glance at her mother. "I saw you, you know—beating sense into that old man. Speaking of which, why *were* you beating an old man with a staff?"

Dahti laughed and explained. By the end of it, a peculiar look had settled on the woman's face. "What? What's wrong?"

"You're so…" Ellen shook her head. "You were so into it that while you were speaking, I forgot it wasn't real, you know?"

The words were somewhat jarring and she froze for a moment. It was funny how she could sit there, summoning benches and food out of thin air, and yet still feel as if the world around her was completely real. She shook her head. "It starts to feel very real."

"More real than I thought." The other woman held one hand out. "I can *feel* the wind."

"I know." She pointed to the water. "Go wade."

Ellen took her lemonade with her and held her robes out of the way—apparently also forgetting that this wasn't real. She shrieked with delight when the water first swirled around her feet and for a moment, her mother could almost see her as she had been as a child, always climbing and exploring. Of all of her children, she had always been the one who was most easily delighted by the world.

It made her life now all the more sad. After the divorce six years before, she had been talked into dates once or twice but she had never allowed herself to get close to anyone. With her children off on their own now, the family had hoped things would change, but they hadn't.

She caught Dahti watching and raised a brow curiously. "Your face looks weird. Or is that merely how...troll faces...look?"

"I am an *orc*," she said with great dignity. "And I was thinking of you as you were when you were a child."

"Oh." Ellen looked self-conscious for a moment. "Sometimes, I think I must have been a nightmare. I remember asking questions about *everything*."

"You did," she said with a chuckle. "But it wasn't a nightmare. It was lovely."

"Are you sure?" The woman looked doubtful. "Because Howie always said—"

"Howie was an asshole," she said bluntly.

Her daughter deflated and came to sit next to her on the bench. "I know," she said. "I can't believe I wasted so many years with him."

"He wasn't an asshole at the start." She patted Ellen's knee. "There were some good years, I think. You two were happy for a while. Then, he simply went off the rails."

"Didn't he?" She rolled her eyes. "He went off to stay in a Buddhist monastery a while back. The kids told me. I wonder if he finally 'found himself' there."

Dahti smiled into her lemonade. "I'd make fun of him, but I'm living in a virtual world so I don't think *I* have much of a leg to stand on."

"Yeah, but you're doing it to help people in comas," Ellen pointed out. "Howie was merely a self-obsessed...douche." *Who cheated on me,* was the end of the sentence she didn't say. She sighed. "I miss being married, though."

"What do the kids think about it?"

"They keep telling me to date. It seems like an awful lot of trouble, though."

"If you miss being married, you'll have to choose at some point between that and the trouble," she told her smartly.

"I know, I know." The woman leaned back. "Hey. I think this is one of the best conversations we've had in years." She straightened and looked around. "Simply a glass of lemonade at the seashore."

Dahti smiled. "You know, I think it is. Let's explore."

"It sounds good to me." Ellen pushed to her feet. "What do you think is around here?"

"Old ruins, maybe? Statues?"

"Really big spiders."

She looked at the sky. "No spiders."

"Fine, but what a baby."

Dahti stifled a laugh and she and Ellen strode into the forest nearby. There was a path—not incredibly obvious, but a place slightly easier to walk than everywhere else. She was fairly sure it hadn't been there before and she felt a certain warmth in her chest at the thought of Prima helping them have a good time together.

Guilt wormed coldly within her and Dahti shied away from the truth. She hadn't liked to hang out with Ellen since the divorce. As the months passed and the woman remained bitter, she had withdrawn. They all had.

She didn't intend to say anything until she thought of Rashat, the silent village, and the children raised knowing about a terrible past and told never to speak of it.

Could she face a dragon and still not have the courage to apologize to her daughter? She shook her head at the thought. What a coward she was.

"Ellen." She stopped and turned and her companion ran smack into her. "Sorry."

"By doze," Ellen said thickly. She wrinkled her face. "Wow, they make this world realistic, don't they? I wouldn't have thought that necklace could stab me." There was a faint trickle of blood on the tip of her nose now. "Um…I won't wake up like this, will I?"

"No! No, no…I'll check." Dahti moved reflexively to pat her pockets for a handkerchief but of course, she had neither handkerchief nor pockets. "I'm sorry."

"It's okay." The woman wiped her nose. "At least no one will see me like this and even if they do, you look weirder."

"We're in orc territory, missy. *You're* the one who looks unusual." Dahti looped her arm through Ellen's—more difficult than usual, given their new height differential—and strolled beside her. She cleared her throat awkwardly. "Um…so, before I managed to stab you in the nose, I wanted to apologize."

"You know, instead of apologizing first, you could have simply not stabbed me."

"I wanted to apologize for something else." Dahti nudged her with an elbow. "I…don't think I was the best mother after you and Howie divorced."

Ellen went silent. When she looked at her daughter, she stared determinedly into the forest but there was a certain set to her chin that let her know she'd been right.

Dammit.

"I thought…well, by that time, your father had passed away, of course," she said awkwardly. "And I thought—well, it isn't important."

"No. I want to hear." Ellen still didn't look back. She tripped slightly over a root and her eyes narrowed in displeasure. Irritated, she shook her head at the indignity and continued with her chin up, not looking at her. "Tell me," she said.

"I…well…I'd lost a spouse, too," Dahti said. "And I think in my mind, I thought I had made my peace with your father's death and you should make your peace as easily with the divorce. But I see now that they weren't the same, not at all."

Ellen started to retort, then bit her tongue. "I shouldn't compare it to Dad *dying*."

"He'd lived a full life, Ellen. He had children he adored, a career—"

"A wife he loved—" she interjected softly and squeezed her mother's arm.

She smiled. "All those things. We knew he didn't have all that long and were able to say goodbye in a different way. There was no…lying. Betrayal. I didn't have to wonder if I could have done anything differently."

Ellen looked like she was going to cry.

"And it doesn't matter what was harder," she said. "What matters is that you were in pain and I wasn't there for you."

Finally, her daughter looked at her. There was something magical about this forest, she thought. Maybe it was the fact that they both knew it wasn't real—the sunlight, the birds, and the rustle of the leaves. Being in a magical dream-world let them speak more honestly than they might have otherwise.

"I wallowed," Ellen said frankly.

"You're allowed," she told her. "Forty years is a bit much, but some wallowing is fine."

"Forty—what?"

"Oh." She waved a hand. "I thought of the orc in the village. Ellen, I never wanted another marriage. Maybe you won't, either. Or maybe you will. Either way, all I want is to see you *happy* before—"

The speed with which her throat closed around those words was shocking. Dahti was there in a make-believe place and she could not feel the pain in her stomach or taste the metal on her tongue. Still, even trying to say the words "before I die" was enough to make her stomach twist.

She'd heard that some people were at peace when they died. Harry certainly seemed to be. She wasn't there yet.

Ellen was crying now and she moved to draw her close to hug her. The woman's shoulders shook, and it took her a moment to realize she wasn't only crying but she was also laughing.

"Ellen?"

"It's…" Ellen gave a hiccupping sob and wiped her eyes. "You're saying all these nice things and you're *dying*, Mom, and I don't know what to do without you. But you went to hug me and you look like Shrek."

Now, Dahti began to laugh and once she started, she couldn't stop. The two women leaned over, clutched their sides, and howled with laughter.

"It's…it's only—" Ellen tried to say, but she dissolved into peals of laughter in the next minute. "Oh, God, it was such a shock. That *face*."

"I told them." She gasped. "I said…I wanted to go *whole-hog*." She gestured at the tusks and both of them lost it again.

When they recovered a couple of minutes later, soft hammocks had appeared in a nearby clearing and the faint sounds of music filled the air. They scrambled in and lay watching the sun shining through the leaves and listening to the waves.

"I'm glad you get to be here," Ellen said. "It's peaceful."

Dahti snorted. "Not always."

"And whose fault is *that*?" Her daughter raised her head. "I saw that fight with the other orc. You were giving him what-for, and it sounded like he wasn't the one who started it."

She decided not to answer.

"It's kind of fun," she mused, "to see my mother acting like a teenager, running into danger and picking fights and all that. Much more fun than watching my *kids* do it, that's for sure." She stretched to catch her fingers. "Thank you, you know. For apologizing. I never thought…you'd think that way."

"Things change," she said. "Maybe this whole experience gave me more courage." She squeezed Ellen's fingers. "I mean it, you know, pumpkin. Be happy."

"I will," Ellen said. "I will. And I'll *definitely* come watch when you defeat the dragon."

CHAPTER SIXTEEN

Dahti woke the next morning to a bucket of seawater that was colder than it had any right to be. She sat up, spluttered, and swung at Rashat, who stood several feet away.

Of course, he didn't need to hold a bucket to pour seawater on someone.

She glared at him. "*One* of those twelve hells is filled with people like *you.*"

"Up." He didn't seem to particularly care that she hated him. "And don't bother to change. You'll merely get soaked again."

"What a fantastic day," she managed to say. She retrieved her staff and followed him into the predawn stillness. He had already begun to stride quickly toward the ocean. "It's still *dark.*"

Now, he favored her with a smile over one shoulder. "You're the one who said forty years was long enough."

"Okay, maybe forty years and a few extra hours."

"Will you complain the whole time we do this?"

Dahti shut up, but she sensed that Rashat didn't exactly dislike the banter. He seemed oddly smaller today, for some reason. Not that he wasn't still absurdly tall and broad-shouldered—especially for a man in his seventies or eighties—but he didn't seem to carry as much with him.

The speed of the change was a little unsettling.

"Are you sure…" she said tentatively.

"Yes?"

"That everything is okay? Yesterday was a day of rather large revelations."

"Maybe for you," he said. "There was only one for me."

"Oh?" They had arrived at the shore and she looked briefly at him. The view of the ocean was astoundingly black, completely unrelieved by moonlight or cities along the coast. In fact, she couldn't tell where the coast *was*.

"I hated them for placing the burden of saving them on my shoulders alone," Rashat told her simply and linked his hands behind his back. He wore new robes, she saw now, not the tattered old shirt and pants he'd worn the day before. "And I hated myself for failing. It galled me to know that every little child in the village learned of that failure. I told myself I deserved it, that a lifetime of pain might even the ledger before the gods called me home. But I still wondered why any true god would do what this one did, and I wondered why it was fair to say I was the only one who failed that day."

She nodded.

"And so it was a revelation," he said quietly, "to find out that another person thought the same. It was as if a weight had been lifted from me. The thoughts were not simply mine."

"No," she said. "They are not only yours. Many shamans have thought as you do. I think your kind have long been deceived by the dragons, and you will triumph against them together."

"Perhaps we will." He had withdrawn within himself again, but the mask he wore now was only of the teacher, not one to hide pain. "It depends whether you can master these techniques, doesn't it? Come this way. Now sit."

"In the water?" Dahti asked.

"Yes. That's the point." He waited and the water swirled around his robes until she finally handed him her staff and sat cross-legged on the sand.

It was only a moment before the next wave rushed in. It broke over her lap, rocked her back, and dragged away. And somehow also left sand in her pants. She looked at her lap in time to catch another wave. This one splashed into her face and she spluttered.

Rashat said nothing. He stared studiously at the ocean but amusement seemed to roll off him in waves.

"Okay," she said and prayed inwardly for civility. "Now what?"

"Just sit," he said.

And so she sat. Wave after wave rolled in and rocked her back and then forward. The level of the water rose until it was above her waist and the waves broke at her shoulders and her chin. She felt a stirring of misquiet. The undertow was more pronounced now and sometimes, she had to flail in an undignified manner to hold her position. At other times, the waves followed one after the other and she managed to get seawater up her nose.

She was *not* a fan of that. It stung, for one thing.

The water wasn't very cold but it was still colder than she was, and it wasn't more than an hour or so before her teeth were chattering.

"So..." She shivered violently. "What am I doing, exactly?"

"Experiencing," Rashat said at length. He looked at the sea like an old friend. "We will also do this in the stream and in the mountain pools."

Another wave caught her across the face. "I don't know if you're aware, but I've been gone for a week and every *day*, the fire dragon may be planning to kill the village."

"If you would like to return sooner and die, you may do so." He looked at her. "I will find another apprentice to teach and when we are finished with our god—"

"You won't defeat your god with water magic."

"Very well, then. Do you have any other ideas or do all of them involve your needless death?"

"I wouldn't call saving a village a 'needless death.'"

"It will be if you do *not* save them and die in the attempt instead." Rashat fixed her with a stern look. "Tell me of the injuries the god suffered."

"A dagger covered in frost was plunged between two of its spinal ridges, it was hurt on one side with earth magic, and one shoulder and another wing were damaged and torn."

"Then we have time," he said. "A god heals no faster than you or I."

"Some gods *they* are," Dahti muttered.

"Snideness and jokes will not help you here," he said sharply. "What *will* help you is learning water magic. I cannot defeat a fire god on my own—or, at least, I do not like my chances."

She sighed. "Well, what am I learning about water now?"

"What are you *not* learning?" he asked philosophically. He held a hand up as the next wave crashed in and it met an invisible wall in front of her. The waters parted to slide around her. She felt the drag of it and the slight settling into the sand. "Earth…well, I have not thought as much on the earth. But water *lives*. That is the difference."

"The earth lives," she retorted. "Rock moves below the surface, cradles new life, and shifts in earthquakes. You cannot tell me you are so naïve as to believe water is the only living element."

He stared at her. "I…that is what our teachers always told us." He held a hand up. "Yes, I am aware there may have been lies among those teachings. Let me…think on it." He paused, although only for a moment. "But water *does* live. To summon the power of it, you must know in your bones how it feels when it crashes, when it flows, and when it falls from the sky. I was raised in this water and I still had to sit here for weeks before my teacher believed I had learned enough."

Dahti looked down and nodded. She knew better than to argue on this point.

It was cold, though—blastedly cold. She thought back to her journey from Berghold to Insea. During the first few days, they had been in the mountains and there had been snow all around them, falling into their boots, and cold seeping up through their bedrolls.

This was a different kind of cold. It ached in her bones instead of stinging on her skin.

With a sigh, she thought of Insea, warm and pleasant, but that memory was not enough to warm her. No, for warmth, she wanted to go back to Berghold where it was underground and safe, filled with chatter and mugs of spiced ale served alongside piping hot sausages and potatoes.

Her thoughts traveled farther still, to the liquid-rock magic of the first dwarven mages, to the absolute, impossible, crushing heat of it, only the smallest part of which she had seen in Mountain's Shadow when the fire worm rose from its slumber—

An exclamation caught her attention and she opened her eyes to a cloud of steam. She flapped her hands to try to dissipate it, caught a wave in the face, and tumbled in the resulting undertow until Rashat hauled her out of the water. He pulled his hand free of her skin with a hiss.

"What did you *do*?" he demanded.

"Nothing!" Dahti shook her head. "Nothing, I swear. I was merely remembering...well, things."

"*What* things?"

"Berghold, and the snow, and the ale..." She remembered most orcs hadn't been to Berghold. "We guarded a caravan that went there. I was thinking of things to keep me warm and I remembered seeing a book about *their* earth magic and how it encompassed the heart of the earth, the rock so hot it glows red and white like iron in a forge..."

Her voice trailed away as she realized what she'd said. She

looked at her clothes, which were now completely dry, and felt the warmth running through her in a comforting rush.

"Oh," Dahti said.

"Indeed." Rashat stared at her with something between resignation, fury, and grim satisfaction. "And it seems you have an affinity for that kind of magic, wouldn't you say, earth orc? For the place where earth meets…fire?"

"I…guess so." She shrugged.

He looked heavenward as if praying for patience. "Does it occur to you," he said finally, "that a god of water, slumbering in the deeps, might be well-attuned to threats?"

She shook her head and shrugged again. "I…guess. Um…well, you know more than I do, and you say that you've been careful not to do anything near the water because it might draw him out." She looked at him and grimaced. "So he might sense us."

"He might." Rashat now looked as if he was seriously contemplating throttling her. The earring on his tusk, now replaced, glinted in the first light of dawn. "Especially since you *used fire magic* in his domain."

"Oh!" She clapped a hand over her mouth. "Oh. *Oh.*"

He gestured as if to say, *see?*

"He'll have sensed me," she said. She looked hastily at him. "Rashat, I'm so sorry. I never thought I could do anything like that, and—"

He waved a hand dismissively and seemed to have shed his anger as quickly as it had come. "It solves one problem," he said finally.

"And what's that?" she asked.

"I wasn't sure how we would find him when the time came," he said. "Now, I have an idea. That is, of course, if he doesn't appear before we're ready and slaughter us all. Come along. We still have streams and ponds to cover and we now have a god possibly hunting us."

CHAPTER SEVENTEEN

Ellen woke to light stabbing into her eyes. She winced, made a noise of complaint, and realized how much she had to pee. She sat bolt upright.

Amber, who seemed to recognize the facial expression, removed the connectors in record time and waved her to a thankfully close bathroom. When she emerged, she was given a tentative thumbs-up, which she returned.

"Good, good," the engineer said and smiled at her. "Did you have a good time?"

"*Such* a good time." She shook her head. "I had no idea it was so…*real.*"

Nick spun in his chair. "You know, it brings up a really good question of what reality *is*—"

"No, no, no," Amber said. "No, no. No. *No.* No Plato's Cave."

He stuck his tongue out and went back to work.

Ellen raised an eyebrow. "Was this going to be some thought experiment?"

"Bingo," Amber said. "Would you like coffee and a snack?"

"*Yes.*" Ellen felt like she could eat a mid-sized horse and still have room left for a nice chocolate cake. "I don't know why I'm so hungry when I've simply been lying there."

"Interpreting a new source of information can be tiring on the body," Amber explained. She hesitated, then added, "Also…stress. I want you to know we didn't eavesdrop and only kept an eye open for signs of distress, but we noticed that your cortisol levels were quite high." Seeing her confused expression, she continued. "Cortisol is a hormone the body produces when someone is stressed. In a natural environment, it would mostly be seen during a predator attack or something, but we made sure that didn't happen during your visit. So it would be…you know…uh, emotional stress." For good measure, she repeated, "We *weren't* eavesdropping. I merely want you to know that if you're tired and hungry, that might be part of it."

Ellen said nothing as they emerged from the hallway into a break room. A large coffee machine had icons for everything from flavor shots to certain amounts of foam, a pile of donuts and muffins rested under a glass dome, and in the corner stood something she hadn't expected to see.

"A popcorn machine?" she asked.

"DuBois," the other woman said with wry fondness. "He's the lead scientist on this project and he *lives* on popcorn. You think I'm making a joke but I'm not. I seriously have no idea how the man doesn't have scurvy. But do feel free to have some if you like. He's always asking us to try it."

"I, uh…maybe another time." Her attention was fixated on the donuts.

"You can have one, you know." Amber gestured at them. "Now, what kind of coffee would you like?"

"Plain black, please."

"Dark roast, light roast?"

"I have no idea. Whatever you think would be best. And I really shouldn't have a donut." Ellen looked at her stomach. "At my age, I can't eat the way you youngsters do and still stay thin."

"You know," the engineer said contemplatively, "your mother mentioned something similar. Well…in a way. When she first got here, we asked if she had any requests. We thought it would be something like riding a dragon, or being Indiana Jones, or something like that. But what she said was—" She took the cup of coffee and put it in front of Ellen at a table. "She wanted to be ugly. She said she'd spent so much of her life going to bed hungry and worrying about her looks, and she merely wanted to…live her life." She punched a set of buttons for a cup of coffee for herself.

Ellen took a sip of the brew, which was delicious, and raised an eyebrow. "What's your point?"

"Well, it's enough to make you wonder, isn't it?" Amber asked. She leaned against the counter and gestured at herself. She wore a man's waffle-knit shirt and jeans over heavy boots. "Part of the reason I dress like this is that it shuts people up about how I look, you know? If I wear a nicer shirt or a dress, they want me to wear makeup, too. If I wear makeup, then it's heels. If I wear heels, they tell me I could stand to lose a few pounds. I have other things I want to focus on."

She still wasn't entirely sure where this was going but leaned back in her chair, though, when Amber took a donut out and put it in front of her.

"What I'm saying," the woman explained bluntly, "is that we'd get a hell of a lot more done in this world if we stopped spending all our energy on how we looked. Your mother is now fighting dragons and defeating traitorous diplomats. And…well, part of that is because there's magic in that world, but you see what I mean."

"Hmm." Ellen looked hungrily at the tempting confectionery. "I'll think about that."

"Do," Amber advised. She settled with her cup of coffee and seemed about to say something more but decided against it.

"Have any of the other people been like that?" Ellen asked. "You know, wanting to be ugly or whatever."

"We don't have enough data yet to say," Amber said. "Your mother is the second official test subject. With Justin, it was imperative that he be in his own body—we didn't want to add the X-factor of him getting attached to a different avatar."

"Huh," she said and shook her head. "Well, whether it's the tusks or the—oh, God, the *smell*—my mother's changed more than a little."

"Has she?" The woman pushed her chair back to lean on the back two feet. She looked intrigued now.

"*Yes,*" she said vehemently. "Even a few months ago, I couldn't imagine her apologizing for…well, anything. She'd always say she did the best she could and she'd do the best she could in the future. It wasn't a lie. She *did* always do the best she could but sometimes, what you need is an apology. And today, I got one from her." She looked at her coffee. "I don't know how to feel about that."

Amber sighed. "Look, I don't know your mother nearly as well as you do, but is it possible that…well, I don't know—that the cancer is part of it?"

"Oh, I think so." She pressed her lips together. It was still difficult to acknowledge that her mother was dying. She gave a little cough to clear her throat. "But I do think part of it is the game. She's…changed. She honestly has." She saw the troubled look on Amber's face. "What's wrong?"

The woman scratched her head. "I'm not sure. I'm…what's the term for it? Borrowing trouble. This is only the second time this has happened and it's not something we bargained on."

Ellen felt a reactive wave of the fear she'd felt the first time she heard about her mother's plan. "What do you mean?" she asked before she could stop herself.

"Comas can change people," Amber said hastily. "*Any* experience changes people. Have you ever read a book that inspired you?"

"Yes, but—"

"This is like that," the engineer told her. "But more, somehow. It's like…people aren't only inspired to be the people they've always wanted to be, they get to try being those people—and when they wake up, the change is made."

"Maybe we should all do that for a while," Ellen said with a little laugh.

When she looked up, though, Amber's face was worried.

"We've seen it in two people," she said. "One who chose to come here to give us data we desperately needed—someone who we already knew was altruistic. And one who was, to be fair, an unknown. But two people aren't nearly enough to decide about this."

Ellen looked at the donut and decided to take a bite before she answered. It was good—it was absurdly good. Diatek didn't skimp on snacks either.

Then again, she was also very hungry.

"I think you *are* borrowing trouble," she said. "And before you tell me that you know more about this than I do, remember that I'm the one who went off the deep end about my mother choosing to be in this world to start with."

Amber took a sip of her coffee. "What made you change your mind?"

"She's…" She searched for the words. "I think she's more *herself* than I've ever seen her. Okay, she's seven feet tall now and has tusks, but even so. That's a weird way to describe someone, but it is…*wait.*" She caught Amber's hand. "I have an idea. I think Mom would like this."

She explained in a hushed whisper, and when she was done, the engineer was smiling.

"You know, I think that would be a good idea. I do think she would like that. Let's go tell the others."

They finished their coffee and donuts quickly—more quickly than the excellent donuts deserved, Ellen thought—and hurried down the hallway to the lab.

Once Jacob, Nick, and DuBois had been briefed and also approved, Ellen left with a cheery wave and a promise to be back. She had a mission that would involve all her siblings and extensive digging through attics and storage units.

Out in the sunlight, she considered the conversation she'd had with Amber. In truth, she was not quite sure how to explain her changed opinion of the game. She had been furious at the thought of losing the last few months she had with her mother.

What she had received, instead, was the chance to see her mother as a young woman—or as a person beyond age or looks. She had the chance to watch her mother fight an old orc with a stave, which she would never in a million years have thought was something she would see. And she'd had one of the best conversations she could remember.

The apology still reverberated in her chest.

The divorce had been beyond difficult, and there had been thousands of times since then that she doubted herself—for the myriad of choices she had made before her husband left her, for her ability to raise children if she could not even make a marriage work, for her looks, and for her lack of a career. But the truth was, she had always tried not to question those thoughts. She was afraid to bring them into the light and study them.

Her greatest fear was the path she might go down if she spent time looking at them.

Now, she thought she might have done herself and her family a disservice. If she'd been courageous enough to sort through those thoughts earlier, maybe she would be in the same place her mother was in now.

Or maybe, she thought, with a small smile, there was no use wondering about the past. The game had changed her mother, and the change was rippling outward.

Either way, she would stop on the way home and buy herself another donut.

CHAPTER EIGHTEEN

Huwat sat back on his feet and wiped his forehead. The caves that made up the shamans' retreat were an excellent place to forage for mushrooms and root vegetables, but both were getting harder to find these days.

Not only that, it grew hotter and hotter.

There was no denying it. Since the god had first emerged from the mountain and then withdrawn to lick its wounds, each day in this place had been progressively warmer. It now seemed to be the height of summer instead of early spring.

There was no question about where the heat came from either. At dawn and dusk, they could see the god pacing the top of the mountain. It never flew but it seemed to want to let them know it was there.

Or maybe it was looking for them.

The shaman wasn't sure. He still wasn't sure that it had seen where they all hid, but he had kept the village on the move since then. Each day, they sheltered in a new place, preferably one with a hill or an oasis between it and the mountain.

And each day, he came back with one or two others to forage

for more food. That was now the entirety of the tribe's existence —searching for food and shelter.

It was miserable.

He had been raised to revere fire, so the concept of fearing heat itself was distasteful to him. Indeed, part of him was grateful to exist in such warm times and witness the pure majesty of the fire god. The other part, however, wanted nothing more than to have gone with Dahti so that he could meet Rashat and see the ocean, that mythical mass of water as wide as the plains.

Huwat could not picture it.

Wearily, he picked his basket up and moved to the next patch of dirt. His back was aching, yet another curse of growing old.

Dahti was a strange one. Of that there was no doubt. He had never met an orc like her and he didn't expect to again. Every day, more out of a sense of duty than anything else, he had prayed for wisdom about her. Was she simply the prophet of a truth none of them wanted to see or was she a trickster, a liar who was testing their faith?

What was odd was that he didn't doubt her. It was exactly like a trick from the old stories for a stranger to show up and whisper your darkest fears, but he didn't doubt her at all.

The truth was, he had selfishly been grateful that he lived in a time with no gods. He prayed to the mountain at dawn and dusk. He offered the sacrifices every year and led the village in their chants. He instructed the little ones to give thanks to the god for their food and to be ready to sacrifice themselves, but the words stuck in his throat every time and he always hoped he would not live to see a god in the flesh.

Because it was a bad bargain. A god who gave the beasts of the earth, only to demand the blood and suffering of mortals, was simply a powerful being playing a cruel joke. Oh, there were many ways to make it sound important and preordained, but none of them rang true.

If a being could give life and if it had the power to do such things, what right did it have to demand their children in return? They had never asked for the bargain.

Huwat learned very early on that the other shamans had asked the same questions—and that none of them wanted to entertain the thought any longer. All of them in living memory had decided to simply bow their heads and give in. It wasn't fair and it wasn't right, but it was the way things were.

And, after all, how long had it been since the god demanded a sacrifice?

He was surprised only by how fervently he'd clung to those beliefs when Dahti had first challenged him. Without realizing it, he had become exactly like his mentor, an old orc of few words and curt instructions. Oh, he was kinder and more liable to discuss the matters of faith with the village, but he also leaned heavily on his status as the shaman to keep them from peering too deeply into the mysteries of the gods.

Because he had always known, deep in his heart, that those mysteries were lies.

Now, he had to face the uncomfortable truth that he'd spent his life defending the very being who had preyed on them for all these years. Somehow, he had been lulled into complacency and had become invested in the Way Things Were. When he was younger, he could have excused it by saying he valued the knowledge of the elders.

When he *became* an elder, he simply asked them not to question it when he told them that the way things had always been was the way they should always be.

The shaman shook his head and looked at the meager contents of his basket. He was getting lost in thought and the tribe would be waiting for supplies. Like it or not, he had angered a god and now, he must keep the villagers as safe as he could.

Once, the orcs had roamed freely across their land. They had not been tied to villages or been separated into tribes. Their songs and their traditions had been shared. There were even legends—only spoken once to him and in a hushed whisper—of a great city his people had built.

These false gods had chained them.

The truth angered him and he growled low in his throat. He might be a shaman, not a warrior or a hunter, but he was still an orc. He knew the urge to fight and tear and slash and wanted this false god ended, and he would be happy only when he stood on its corpse.

Huwat knew he could not do it on his own. He was no Rashat, born with unusual powers, and had been like most children—feckless and silly. Perhaps a little more interested in the old legends but not enough to be noteworthy. It was only one night, when he decided to break all the rules of the village and climb the mountain, that he had been chosen as the shaman's apprentice.

His hands stilled at their work. It had been so long since he'd thought of that night.

It was still—not a year for locusts and no winds ruffling the plains grasses. No clouds, either. He had been restless all day, barely able to sit still, so energetic that even a hunt hadn't tired him, and he knew he wouldn't be able to sleep.

What possessed him to climb the mountain, he couldn't say. He knew only that his feet were on the hillside and his hands scrabbled for holds in the rock, and he didn't even look back to see if the watchmen saw him.

There wasn't a path, but that didn't bother him. No one climbed the mountain, after all. It was forbidden.

Far from becoming more tired as the climb went on, he only felt more alive. If he were to go out onto the plains, he was sure he could run forever. He could climb the tallest tree or fight a lion barehanded. The thoughts teased fleetingly at him, but not for long. He was too absorbed with how he felt and with the way he wanted to burst out of his skin.

When he saw the fire, he was so surprised he almost fell off the mountainside.

His first thought was to attack. No one should be there. Then, of course, he remembered that *he* should not be here, either.

And the fire was so beautiful. It was like nothing he'd ever imagined and as if all the fire he had seen was only a dream and this was real.

"Huwat," a voice said and he realized that the shadowy shape by the fire was the shaman.

Who had recognized him.

There was no going back, but more than that, he could not have walked away from that fire if he had a hundred horses trying to drag him. His feet brought him irresistibly to it.

"You heard the call," the shaman said shortly.

"Call?" He could only see the flames.

"You felt the fire's magic stirring in your blood." This was, perhaps, the most words Huwat had ever heard him say at one time. "You came to find it."

He gaped at him. "*That's* why I'm here?"

"Yes. It is time to find an apprentice." The shaman gestured to him. "It is you. You will be shaman after me."

"But—"

Huwat was not sure he wanted this. There was a girl in the village, one whose smile made him feel like he was turning inside out. He'd thought of impressing her with his kills in the hunt.

The shaman let the flames die and as quickly, his strange energy was gone. "We begin training tomorrow," the elder said. "At dawn. Get some sleep." He set off down the mountain without waiting for him to follow.

That had been it. There had been no choice and no discussion. Huwat bowed his head. He had been summoned to this life. Perhaps that was why he told stories of others being summoned to fates *they* did not want.

It was a useless train of thought. He stood and a shout caught his attention.

He dropped the basket of mushrooms and ran as fast as his

old legs would take him. There were more shouts now from the others who had come with him. When he emerged from the caves, they looked at him in fear.

They did not need to say why.

The god still could not fly well. That much was apparent. But it did not need to. It now slunk down the side of the mountain and directly toward the camp the villagers had made.

CHAPTER NINETEEN

"Go!" Huwat called to one of the others. "Make sure the villagers have seen."

They should have, certainly. There were watches posted now but it was too big a risk to not make sure.

The others looked at him and he knew he would say what they most feared. He drew himself tall—he was still the shaman, after all—and commanded them firmly. "You two, come with me. We must stand between our village and the god."

They wavered. Of course, he thought, they would. Mortals did not go easily to their deaths, after all, and these had so recently learned that their beliefs might well be lies. Of course, when he ordered them to go into battle, they would waver.

But they did not have time for that right now.

"I am not telling you to fight the god for glory or faith," he said simply. "I am telling you to do so because our kin are in that camp and they will certainly die if we do not fight for them."

That steeled them to what must be done. They followed him through the grass, cutting a path toward where the god approached, low on its belly like a large cat on the prowl. They did not try to avoid being seen. With any luck, he thought, it would think the villagers were still in the warren of caves.

Any time they could buy was of the essence. He was honest with himself that he did not see himself triumphing in this fight.

Every day they live is a triumph. It must have been his thoughts as the words were inside his head, but he swore he was not the one who had thought it.

Was it the guidance of a god? A true god? Huwat did not know, but he felt courage fill him nonetheless. Although this was a beast of fire and his magic would never truly undo it, he was not powerless.

"Flank it," he said to the two villagers with him. "As much as you can, stay out of sight. Watch the tail—it can swing quite powerfully. Trade off if you can—one of you go in to land a strike while the other hangs back."

"What can we do against it?" one of them asked him bleakly. He held his spear up. It was stone-tipped and finely made, but he was right that it looked ridiculous next to the beast.

"Listen to me," he said. He wanted to stop and face them but they could not take the time. "We know it as a god, but it is no more than a beast like any other. You've fought your share of enemies and you will defeat this one in the same way. Its flesh can be reached through the scales. It has tendons, muscles, and skin."

"Eyes," one of them said.

Huwat hesitated. "Yes, but…leave its face to me."

They accepted a little too eagerly, and he hid his sigh. When it came down to it, they would fight for their families but he might well be dead by then.

All must die in their own time. He smiled ruefully. His only regret was that he had not trained an apprentice. He'd hoped Dahti would have met that need.

She would not be an apprentice of *his* tradition. When this was over, however, they might not have anything left that he recognized as tradition. Perhaps the young ones would be best served by finding their own way through magic as well as faith.

Oddly, that gave him courage. *The old must die so the new can flourish.* That was one of their teachings. Perhaps it had been meant to guide him in this very moment. Who could say?

The dragon had seen them now. Its black-and-red eyes were fixed on them. Smoke billowed from its nostrils and the ground smoldered under its feet. He knew it was only a matter of luck that the entire plains had not caught fire yet.

What was it the human had called this god? Huwat searched his memory for the unfamiliar term.

Ah, yes.

He smiled grimly as he strode forward. "Hello, worm."

His voice carried on a rising wind and the god crouched with a hiss. A growl began in its throat, low and hypnotic. It began to move with menace in every tiny ripple of its muscles.

"What did you call me?"

"I called you a worm," Huwat said. "For that is what you are, is it not? You are not a god."

"What is a god?" Now, it sounded amused. "A greater being than a mortal."

"You are mortal," he said. He hoped it was true. It was purely a gamble. "You can be wounded and you can die."

Whatever instinct told him to throw himself sideways as soon as he spoke, he was grateful for it—the grasses nearby erupted in flames so hot and bright that they did not even spread. The mere moment of the heat blistered the side of his face.

He scrabbled to his feet and dove sideways once more, this time onto the burned ground. His hope was to outwit the god —*worm*, he reminded himself—but to his surprise, he heard it hiss in annoyance. When he looked up, it turned, awkward and ungainly. The two warriors raced away and tried to stay out of sight. One of them must have pushed in close enough to do damage.

The worm blew fire at one flank and then the other. One cry of pain followed but nothing more.

Huwat's stomach twisted. He had no idea if one—or both—was dead, but if not, he needed to draw the creature's attention back to him.

Still unsure what he would do next, he decided he would think of something along the way. Or he wouldn't. Either way, he'd be dead soon enough. He chuckled and shook his head. It was strange what you found funny when you stared death in the eye.

He thumped his staff on the ground and shouted, "Worm! I am not finished."

The dragon's head whipped around and it snarled at him, narrow-eyed. "What do you want, puny one?"

That was a good question. Huwat had nothing planned.

"What is your plan?" he called. "Do you hope for one last meal before my kind hunts you and kills you?"

It breathed fire at him again, but he was already moving. This time, it was not only one blast and he had to keep running until his old knees ached and his lungs burned. Everything smelled of smoke and he could no longer remember which way they were facing. He looked for the mountain that marked the shamans' retreat, but between his smoke-blurred gaze and the beast and the grasses, he could not see it.

The creature howled in pain again and his heart soared. At least one of the guards must still be alive.

When he caught sight of the man, he uttered an audible gasp. Half of the orc's face was blistered, far more badly than his, and some of the skin on his shoulder was blackened.

They might worship fire and thrive in heat, but they were not immune to its dangers. He knew this man should be in the village with salve on the burns and water being fed between his lips every few minutes. But who could say when he would have either rest or healing?

The man lunged again and again, and Huwat had to run to him as the worm gathered its breath once more. The warrior screamed in pain when he dragged him to the ground and hauled him under the worm's belly.

"Where's the other?" he asked, although he was afraid he knew the answer.

The man's stare was bleak. "He ran."

"He *what?*"

"He said to hold him." He looked at the beast that now thrashed its head and twisted to try to see them. "I thought…he was planning to strike at it. Then I saw him running."

Coward. Fury filled Huwat. He looked into the man's eyes. "We *will* hold him," he promised. "And we will find the coward and end him. His line will be finished."

They both knew it was not likely to happen, that this road ended in death for them, but they nodded to one another. Now they had a goal beyond defeating the worm. It was merely a distraction but it brought a measure of comfort.

He gestured to the man to take one flank and ducked under the worm's belly, took careful aim, and drove the ragged edge of his stave onto the massive wing where he could see the still-healing cut.

Its scream deafened him. His ears ringing, he ran. He remembered he should not run in a straight line, but he was fairly sure he was so dazed that he couldn't have done so if he wanted to.

He didn't get far enough. The dragon spun and its tail struck him on the side. The shaman careened away with a long cut under one arm where one of the spines had ripped through his robes. He landed so hard, he thought he bounced.

His cry of pain made him feel ashamed. He was an orc and while he might not be a warrior, an orc was an orc, dammit. Like hell would he die there.

"Still injured, *god?*" he taunted as he found his feet and forced a laugh out of his tortured lungs. "Driven away by a trainee shaman and a *human*?" He said a silent apology to the human, who had done quite good work, all things considered, but old habits died hard. Every orc knew humans were puny, weak, and gutless.

It hissed at him but he saw it limping. He remembered Dahti saying that the human had injured it near the tail and the impact of hitting him this time must have hurt more than it expected. Perhaps there was a way to tell the other warrior to aim at its tail, he wondered but decided not. The man was barely standing as it was. His only chance of success hinged on the element of surprise.

"You know there's nothing left for you," the shaman called. "You did well, all of you, convincing us that you had brought life to the earth and the beasts to our campfires. But the lie had to unravel someday and here we are. So, what'll it be? Will you walk onto the spears of our army or will you try to run?" He bared his teeth. "Because we *will* find you. You missed your chance, *worm*. The shaman has already gone to gather the water shamans, and they are coming for you."

"*Liar!*" It tried to rear into the air and flapped its wings but screamed in pain. "The water tribe was killed for its disobedience."

"One of your kin *tried* to kill the water tribe," he corrected. He saw something out of the corner of his eye and it was all he could do to not look. "It became greedy. It wanted to take something that wasn't its to take, and it not only failed, it showed the rest of us the truth."

The dragon limped away and Huwat saw the flicker again. He narrowed his eyes to focus.

Yes. The warrior who had run was back with others.

Whatever godsdamned, foolish plan they had, he knew he had to keep the god distracted. He began to circle away from where they crept through the grasses.

"The water tribe yet lives!" Huwat called. "As do the rest of us.

Our shamans will join powers as we once did. The call has gone out and there is no stopping it now."

They really *should* have sent messages, shouldn't they? He shook his head at the missed opportunity.

"Your kind…are weak." Its voice was fainter now and weaker.

For the first time, he felt a flicker of hope. He might yet survive this. They all might.

He saw the others waiting for their chance and spread his arms. "How can you say we are weak when you could not kill one old man?"

The worm drew breath to blast him to ashes when the villagers charged. They were silent and uttered no battle cries. Knives or gardening implements and shards of pottery were grasped in every hand. Others carried buckets of water.

As one, they fell on the dragon from behind and began to drive their weapons between its scales. Where they pried the armor away, the others threw water.

The beast's scream now was like nothing he had ever heard. He understood now, in the last moment, how much older a worm could be than an orc. It was as if he could hear the generations of his kind in its last call—the wheel of the seasons, the diversions of earthquakes and wildfires and storms.

The worm was not lying when it said it was stronger than they were.

But they worked together and it had come for them for the last time. It sank into a heap, the light gone from its eyes, and the village erupted with cries of joy. Huwat strode forward to clap the warrior on the shoulder.

"You went to get them."

"You doubted me," the man said with a smile. "I'll not say I didn't think of running and not coming back, but I realized how we might win without a water shaman."

"So you did." He nodded. "Some of you, come with me. We need to bear Gartun to the camp and—"

The cry that came next wasn't so much one they heard with their ears as with their souls. Huwat swore that even the winds stood still for a moment while it pierced the world. It was the embodiment of grief and vengeance.

"What *was* that?" the warrior asked.

"They know," Huwat said quietly. "They know their kin has been killed. They're coming."

All he could hope was that Dahti would be back in time.

CHAPTER TWENTY

The next week passed in a haze.

Perhaps it wasn't a week. It could have been more—or less. Dahti remembered training through the day and sleeping precious little at night. She recalled her clothes being soaked from endless time spent in the water of the ponds, the ocean, and the streams.

Shivering started when she so much as *looked* at a body of water.

While she had never been a fan of dried fish, she grew to hate it with an absolute passion. She also learned that she could hate something and wolf it down at the same time.

And she did all of it in near-silence. The villagers had withdrawn, at Rashat's insistence, into the tunnel between the fire lands and the water tribe's territory. It was the closest thing to safety anyone could think of, but she shuddered to think of them locked in the darkness, prowling endlessly while they listened for the sounds of an angry dragon.

Without them, however, she saw a different side to the shaman. The older orc was not only astute, he was shockingly irreverent—something she could only guess came from decades of living with the ruins of his faith.

Most of the change seemed to be a lightness of being that she could not quite put her finger on. She saw it sometimes in the softness of his face when he looked at the forest or the quiet contemplation with which he fixed the traps.

He always made them start their day with a harvest from the traps. "I'm doing this to save my people," he told her, "not leave them to starve."

She became exceptionally good at filleting fish and hanging them so she could make more of the dried fish she hated so passionately.

In the evenings, he sat in silence and stared into the fire, and it was only partway through their time, when she heard a few notes, that she realized he was recalling the songs he had vowed to take with him to the grave.

Dahti didn't comment on it and over time, he became bolder. The isolated snatches of his low, almost hypnotic hum gave way to full songs and from there, to actual singing. All the songs reminded her of water, whether it was the clear blue of the ocean she had first seen, or the stillness of a forest pond, or the cheerful burble of water over rocks. Once, and only once, he sang a song both powerful and mournful that told the story of a fishing boat lost in a storm and the wreckage washing ashore.

With that one, she hid her face so he would not see her cry. But when she looked up from wiping her eyes, he was watching her and she thought perhaps he approved.

The softness she sometimes saw at the end of the day was matched by the ferocity he showed during training. After the first day, he'd done an abrupt about-face.

Although he still woke her the next morning with ice-cold seawater to the face.

After watching her earth magic, Rashat now encouraged her to hone those skills she had already spent time training in. With the pressure and heat that stone could summon, he seemed to think she might be able to harm the dragon in some measurable way.

She was terrified by the very idea. Although she'd fought elves and dwarves and even a bizarre, black-armored mechanical creature, a dragon was very different. She remembered how big the dragon had been at Mountain's Shadow. It had dwarfed her, and its strength and magic were far beyond her.

Prima, far from being encouraging, was offended. *"Do you think I would set you up for failure?"*

"No," Dahti told her, "but I might have missed an obvious way of getting out of this that you had intended."

"Ah." The AI took a moment to consider this. *"I think you'll be able to do it,"* she said finally. *"People are very resourceful when they have to be."*

Quite honestly, she did not find this particularly encouraging.

She also did not appreciate that she was supposed to strike the most important blows at the water dragon but that her mentor defeated her handily in every sparring match. It seemed she could not so much as finish a spell before her head was encased in water, or she had saltwater in her eyes, or the ground was so slick beneath her feet that she could not stand.

That said, she also could not come up with a better idea than being the one to strike the killing blow.

She should have sent Huwat—a fact she mentioned to Prima sometime after the first week was up. Her mind constantly reminded her that she was good with clouds of dust and hot soil under horses' hooves and little clods of dirt on wolves, but that was nothing compared to a dragon. The shaman, with decades of training in the powers of fire, would have been far better.

When she mentioned this, however, the AI merely snorted. *"If you'd sent Huwat, he and Rashat would still be fruitlessly engaged in an escalating, passive-aggressive series of bows and ceremonial messages and Rashat would not have emerged from his funk."*

"How can you be certain?

"*I made this world. I can see the futures of it. And, before you ask—no, I cannot see this future because you are involved and humans always find a way to surprise me.*"

"There's something to be said for that, I guess," Dahti said.

"*Usually, they surprise me in a stupid way.*"

"Oh, shut up."

"Do you always talk to yourself?" Rashat asked from behind her.

Dahti jumped and turned. "How long have you been standing there?"

"Long enough to hear that you think Huwat would have been a better choice for this." The old orc rolled his shoulders and looked up to where the sun was beginning to drop in the sky. "And perhaps you're right, but you're what we have to work with."

"You should be a motivational speaker," she told him.

"A…what?"

"A…hmm. It's something people do when their culture runs out of big problems."

He stared blankly at her.

"Anyway, since we only have me to work with, should we start on anything in particular?"

"Like you need to ask." Rashat held his hand up and summoned a ball of water that spun lazily. "It's time to spar."

"Oh, not again."

"Yes, again. How do you expect to beat a dragon if you don't practice your magic?"

"I always won before," she muttered. "Battle has a way of… bringing out inventive thoughts." And gruesome ones, of course, but she did not mention that.

"If you don't mind, I'd prefer not to depend on your inventiveness in the moment." The ball of water disappeared into a shower of droplets, and he pointed at the water.

"Oh, not again…" Dahti knew better than to try to change his mind, however. She went to the waterline and sat.

They began each fight with her immersed in a body of water. Rashat claimed that only immersion would give her the understanding she needed to master the element—either as a practitioner or as someone who fought it.

Today, she could have sworn that there was something different in the water, an echo almost like whale song but far less friendly. She listened for it and even slid to duck her head under the surface, and when she came up, he was watching her.

"There's a…sound."

"It's the god." He caught himself on the word. "Beast. It's getting closer."

She froze. Her reflex was to scramble out of the water but she fought it. "You're…simply letting me *sit* here?"

"How small do you think it is? I assure you, it cannot hide in any of these little waves." He was amused now. "You cannot defeat it without understanding it, and you cannot understand it without seeing its home, apprentice. Relax. Concentrate."

Dahti closed her eyes, even though every instinct screamed at her to get out and run without looking back

Water. It billowed away from every motion like air but stronger, pushing her skin into little ripples at times when it passed. It closed her in, pressed around her chest and her stomach, and yet it also lifted her. When she was underwater, she felt as if she were flying at times.

She had just settled, a smile on her face, when Rashat's first strike caught her across the back of the head. The spray of water was so fine and powerful that it felt almost like the cut of a lash. Her eyes snapped open and a wave caught her in the face.

He'd planned that. She knew he had. He'd timed that strike perfectly.

As she turned, she deliberately didn't look at him and simply yanked with all her strength. The ground slid under his feet.

Rashat stumbled and his next strike went wide into the sky. She used the moment to scrabble away on the sand and wiped the water out of her eyes.

"That was a dirty trick," she called.

"This god doesn't fight fair," he responded. "So neither will I."

"Bastard," she muttered. She blasted the dirt in front of him into a spray of fine particles, the same trick she'd used to blind archers who once hunted her, but he wiped the dust away efficiently with a smattering of rain.

They circled one another as their feet splashed in the water and slid in the sand.

Her next attack was a clod of dirt around his feet. It took him a second to wash it away with water, during which time she attached more to his beard and wedged another in one of his ears. He was swearing by the time all of them were out, but he flashed her a smile.

"Now *that's* the kind of annoyance I'm looking for."

Dahti smiled, flushed and pleased by the praise, only to get a jet of water up her nose. She shrieked and swore before she heated the sand under his feet and forced him to dance away. The heat followed him in little pockets that made him curse and hop until an out-of-rhythm wave knocked her off her feet and held her upside down by the ankles.

It dropped her in the next moment and she landed in an ungainly heap. She gave a silent prayer of thanks for her young body as she stood and shook out the pain—only to have the same thing happen a second later. As she stood, swearing this time, Rashat launched a stream of water at her like a fire hose.

That was *enough*. She ducked under the stream of water and attacked. Her shoulder caught him on the thigh and he fell with a surprised "oof" sound she wished she could play on repeat.

She didn't know much about fighting hand to hand, but she had Lyle's advice to guide her until she reached what she wanted —Rashat's staff. She waited until he was a little off-balance as he pushed to his feet before she delivered a punch to his solar plexus.

He toppled again and she leapt over him to sprint to the staff. He yelled as well and she heard him running behind her.

His defense was too late. She swung the staff and he barely managed to get out of the way by dropping into the sand. With it in her hands, he couldn't get close, and if she kept up her flurry of attacks, he couldn't focus well enough to launch any truly impressive spells.

Dahti rained blows on him, kicked him back, and advanced on him with her hands raised for a spell.

It never came. She kicked him in the shins instead and he went over sideways and a wave broke over his head.

"I yield," he said when he stood. He was panting.

Suddenly worried, she put the staff down. She had broken the rules. After all, this was to be a magical fight, and they'd always tried not to physically *hurt* one another. To her surprise, Rashat was smiling.

"Good," he said simply. "*This* was what I wanted to teach you. It was the single greatest turning point in my skill as a shaman, and it is what allowed me to even inflict some damage to the god in its last attack."

She frowned. "I…don't understand. I didn't use magic."

"Precisely," he said. He smiled at her and the earring on his tusk caught the light. "The first failing of many would-be magic users is that they cannot use magic at all. You have passed that barrier. The second failing is that they use magic as the only way to solve problems. It is not, any more than machines can solve every problem. Magic is a tool like any other. You must learn to use it together with things such as weapons in order to triumph."

Her mouth fell open in surprise. "Oh," she said, quite confused. "Oh, I hadn't…I hadn't thought… *Oh.*"

Rashat nodded. "And, with that, I think it is time for dinner."

Dahti's happiness turned to despondency. More dried fish.

Delightful. "Prima," she said under her breath, "remind me next time that I want to be ugly, *not* smelly, and also somewhere with an abundance of good food I get to eat."

"Noted."

The temperature was dropping as the sun dipped in the sky and she shivered as they walked to camp. The villagers had left various supplies but had taken almost everything as, of course, they used what they owned regularly. There was therefore nowhere to get a change of clothing or a spare blanket.

She watched while her mentor went to get them pieces of dried fish, and she was about to suggest that maybe they should eat the fish cooked on a rock when the song she had heard in the water came back to her.

It exploded into the air so loudly that it threw her forward. She pushed up and ran to him. Her ears were not ringing, she knew, which meant the song was inside her head.

"Rashat!"

"Yes." He looked beyond her. "It's here."

Dahti looked over her shoulder at the beast that rose out of the water. It was such a deep blue that she might have mistaken it for black save for the fact that the setting sun lit its iridescent scales. It coiled into motion and swung its head from side to side like a cobra.

She had expected to feel terror when she saw it. To her surprise, however, the word that came out of her mouth was, "Showtime."

CHAPTER TWENTY-ONE

"It's starting!"

Jacob, who had been staring at budgeting spreadsheets, jumped wildly, spilled cold coffee down his front, and almost fell off his office chair. Beside him, Amber gave a whoop, spun twice in her chair, and dashed to the main floor with Nick hot on her heels. Jacob searched for a new shirt, crouched behind his desk to change, and followed.

In the labs, assistants and scientists moved like one well-oiled machine to get seats pulled up at the monitors, while DuBois offered commentary on the unfolding fight. The entire lab had become absorbed in this branch of the story. Passionate arguments were exchanged over whether Dahti should have bothered to try to talk Rashat out of his funk, as well as an in-depth round of betting on everything from the outcome of this fight to the tactics that would be used.

It had been tacitly known that as soon as the fight began, everything in the lab would be put on hold. They were merely lucky, Jacob thought, that it hadn't happened at two AM. He had no doubt that all of them would have taken cabs to the lab to watch.

The PIVOT team members, having been in their offices, were last to the party and thus too late to get seats. They hung out at the back and Amber climbed on one of the lab tables to watch. Unlike Nick and Jacob, she wasn't tall enough to see over peoples' heads.

"The dragon," DuBois announced, "has approximately eight thousand, seven hundred and forty-eight health points."

"Hit points. And...approximately?" Nick muttered. "What's this guy's idea of *exact*?"

Jacob leaned closer. "You went to MIT, Nick. You *know* you never. Ask. A scientist. That."

His friend muffled his laughter into his hand as DuBois went on to explain the spells, rotations, and tactics of each of the fight participants, all with slightly incorrect language.

"One last, *very* important thing," he said.

Everyone dragged their eyes away from the dragon on the screen.

"Who wants popcorn?" the scientist asked.

The water dragon did not look at the two orcs at first. Instead, it investigated its surroundings—the setting sun, the waves, and the scent of the air. Dahti had no idea how it hung in the air as it had no wings that she could see. When she squinted, the air around it seemed to vibrate.

She looked at Rashat and saw his anger rising. When he was her teacher, the shaman had been endlessly patient, always goading her while remaining calm. It was a role he filled quite naturally.

Now, she could see him slipping into the man he had been when she met him—consumed by anger and regret. His composure eroded as he beheld his enemy, the one he had watched slaughter thousands of the water tribe. He seemed younger now with a new adult's fury at an unjust world.

Dahti wanted to tell him he should suck it up—that he should be the shaman his people needed, not the one he'd felt driven to become. She sensed that those were not the words he needed to hear, however. Instead, she looked at him and said simply, "Rashat."

He turned to her but with only a fraction of his focus. The rest was on his nemesis.

"You do not stand alone," she told him.

At that, his expression cleared. He inclined his head at her before he stepped forward and called, "Worm!"

The dragon's head swung toward them. She could feel its focus in the prickling of the hair on her arms. This was a predator, a beast made to rip and shred other beings, both with claws and with mastery of magic, and her instincts knew that.

It moved so quickly that she did not track it through the air. It was before them in an instant, its coils moving slowly as it hung suspended. It lowered its head to sniff at Rashat.

"I remember you," it said at long last. "The little wizard. Your despair tasted…very sweet. I will savor it again today."

"You will not," he said. He was smiling. "You should have killed me when you had the chance, worm. You left me lying half-dead on the beach with the bodies of my friends beside me. You killed our elders, you killed our mothers and fathers, you killed babies in their cradles, and you gorged on our fear, but you made a mistake. You left some of us alive."

The dragon hissed very softly. "Deplete the herd entirely and there would be no second meal."

Dahti clenched her hands. While all she wanted was to scream obscenities at this dragon, she could not draw attention to herself yet. She and Rashat had drawn up a plan and run through it every day, with her adding to it as she learned new things.

Given all the effort they'd put into it, she wouldn't mess it up now.

"You will be nothing," the shaman said. "I will kill you today. The only thing this tribe will *ever* remember of you is how to kill your kind. We will keep your scales in our huts and your skull in the hall of our elders."

It hissed again but this time, it was a laugh. "You are mortal. I am not."

"You can bleed, worm," he said, "and you can die. You are as mortal as I am."

"I feasted on your line before your grandfather was even born," the beast told him. "You and your kin are fleeting, as insignificant as insects that crawl in the dirt. You cannot comprehend my existence. Where you are weak, I am strong. Where you face the world, squinting in confusion, I see clearly. It was not a lie to call myself your god. You *should* worship me. I am utterly beyond you."

"You're forgetting why you came here today," Rashat said. "It wasn't because you awoke hungry in your lair. You came because you sensed a threat. You sensed the presence of fire magic in your territory."

Its coils twisted tightly and a hiss carried the hint of a shriek on the wind. "Such a thing is impossible. Your tribes are mortal enemies."

"Once, we were." He folded his hands in his sleeves. Dahti could see him fighting for calm but he did better than could be expected. "Because you fed us lies about them. But you miscalculated, worm. In your long sleep, we became known as the most pious of the tribes and during your attack on us, when you slaughtered my people, you exposed yourself as a liar. *You* shattered the faith of all the tribes. And while you slept, fat on the blood of my people, we began to learn how to defeat you."

The dragon uncoiled like a cobra and reared skyward.

"Every god demands sacrifices," it boomed. "It is not your place to question my choices!"

"You're right." Power gathered around the shaman's hands. He did not look at her, but she could feel his attention. She nodded where she stood barely visible out of the corner of his eye and saw him smile. To the dragon, he said, "It is my place to end you."

The power that burst forward from them both was crushing —the deep black of water and the hot, close pressure of a mine. Dahti summoned her memories of Berghold and Insea and infused the heat of the mountain's eruption into her magic, while Rashat channeled the icy, crushing force of a waterfall.

The magic struck the enemy on its exposed belly and the skin flared a sickly brown-tinged red. The dragon screamed. A ripple moved along it, power waiting to be expelled. Its jaws opened but neither Dahti nor Rashad was in the way of it any longer.

The jet of water struck the sand and gouged a deep hole. The shockwave of its anger bowled through the air but it did not have the force it would have underwater.

It was a creature out of its element—that was what the two had realized as they planned. Any time a dragon came to feed on the orcs, it had to take itself out of its element and was therefore not as powerful as it would be on its home turf. Its ways of fighting were adapted from where it had grown.

This dragon was used to planning its movement, knowing that the water might carry it far.

Air did not work that way and neither did earth.

Dahti lifted the pile of sand it had blasted away and let it hang in the air. This spell had never worked on Rashat, but the dragon was a creature of the deep, not of the air and the rains. She concentrated, recalled the heat that had radiated off the fire dragon's scales, and as each grain of sand heated cherry red, she flung them at their adversary.

Its scales were close-set and almost impervious to knives or spears but tiny grains of sand could find weak points that no blade could. They clung to the dragon's armor and it writhed in pain, shrieking before it dived into the water to cool the sand and its scales.

She watched its health tick down—slowly, slowly, slowly. The magic had left her in a chunk and she was almost dizzy. What she wouldn't give for one of the magic potions Lyle had carried on their last journey.

They nodded to one another and Rashat was the one whose power greeted the beast when it surged out of the water again. Several jets of water, each tiny and carrying terrible force, struck its scales and belly and arrowed toward the points where she had burned it.

The dragon hissed and screeched, furious now.

"Try to stop me, pathetic mortal. You are bound to this land, and *I*—I am the god of your people!" It streaked away toward one of the islands.

The shaman panted where he had sunk to his knees in the sand and Dahti pulled him upright. The two of them steadied each other as the dragon circled the islands, yelling its rage.

"It dares to be angry," Rashat said with low fury in his voice. "It wanted to kill again, to show me that I could not stop it while it feasted on the island dwellers, and it is angry now that none of them survived its last attack."

"This is why we will end it," she told him. Then, as the dragon turned toward them, she nodded seriously at him. "Now! Run!"

The two of them broke into a sprint. Their feet slipped and slid in the loose sand as they raced to the paths and the village. A hair-raising screech from their adversary told them that it had the scent and reveled in the hunt.

Dahti's magic was running low, and although Rashat's was nowhere close to depleted, he still panted with the effort of using it.

"Waves crashing over rocks," he called to her as they ran,

naming those things native to water that might hurt anything within it, including a dragon.

"Riptides," she called in response.

"Colliding waves!"

"Ice!"

An ominous whistling in the air behind them made both of them shut up and try to use all of their breath and focus to reach the village—and the spear they had left with its tip in the cooking fire.

The dragon swept low over their heads and its claws lifted Dahti by the shirt and shoulders and bowled her over into the dirt. She had a dim vision of its tail catching Rashat and he tumbled as well, but the next moment, she landed hard and pain exploded all across one side.

Using her momentum, she rolled and pushed to her feet. She had learned one thing from sparring. If you waited to feel the pain from a blow, you'd never keep going. In a battle, to stop moving was to die.

The dragon had flung her far past the cooking fire and now turned on the shaman. It cared more about him and wanted its revenge. She was untrained and it knew its powers could drown her in an instant.

But she was not the spring chicken it thought she was and she wasn't about to use magic to solve every problem.

Which gave her an idea.

"Rashat!" Her voice carried easily. "Remember our last sparring session?"

Squared off against the beast, he managed to spare her a glance. She saw it absorb the arrangement of the battlefield—him close to the water, the dragon between him and the firepit, and her behind the fire pit.

"Tidal wave!" she called.

He put the pieces together the same way she had—or, at least, she hoped he did. He gathered his power, and as the dragon reared to strike, he flung every ounce of power he had left.

Dahti had not understood, until that moment, the truth of what he was. She knew that he summoned spells easily, but she had seen any number of talented magic users since she came to this world. When Huwat told her that Rashat did magic as naturally as he breathed, even in the cradle, she had assumed this was an exaggeration.

It was not.

The force of the tidal wave was visible in the air. It stripped the leaves from the trees as it passed and time seemed to slow to a crawl…three more steps to the spear…two more…one more. Her hand extended but her gaze remained fixed on the monstrous wave moving toward her. Somewhere, distantly, she heard the dragon utter a mournful cry.

In the next moment, the wave broke over it and carried it down.

She planted the spear base-first in the ground and watched, open-mouthed in horror, as the creature plunged toward her. She saw her death a thousand times over in that wave.

Huwat, I'm sorry. I pray Rashat will honor his end of the bargain.

The absolute terror of her death struck her and her arms raised more out of instinct than anything else.

The world went black.

Nick, who had sprinted to get popcorn, heard the call of "tidal wave!" from the monitors.

Although he had no idea what was going on, like hell would he miss anything tidal-wave-themed. He sprinted back, popcorn bouncing in his hand, and halfway down the hallway, he heard people draw in their breath and yell to each other about what they thought Dahti was doing. He dropped the popcorn entirely and sprinted as quickly as he could.

The hollow boom of the spell clipped on the speakers. It rippled in the picture, a sonic wave as it hurtled toward the dragon. The coils swayed and lifted as if borne on an unseen current before the wave hit.

"There! Look!" One of the assistants pointed to the bottom of the screen, where Dahti's avatar could be seen planting a spear.

"Holy shit, holy shit, holy shit." Jacob white-knuckled a chair.

"She's not going to—" Amber clapped her hand over her mouth. A few people gave her terrified looks when she broke off.

"Come on," DuBois muttered at the screen. "Come on, Dotty, you've got this." His gaze flicked to the bloodwork monitor. "Spike of cortisol, frontal lobe activity flare—yes!"

Everyone jumped and someone called out as the wave and the dragon crashed onto her. About half the group had their faces hidden in their hands, and every single one of them flinched at the sound of impact.

"It's okay! It's okay!" An assistant skidded to their knees in front of the monitor and pointed to where they had seen her disappear. "Look. Keep watching!"

As the dragon tumbled away, a chunk of its health gone and the burning spear lodged in its side, a boulder was revealed. Everyone held their breath. Nick realized he and Jacob were holding one another's hands so hard that the bones creaked. They both yanked their hands free but Nick couldn't breathe as he waited.

"Come on," he whispered under his breath. "Dahti…"

The boulder shattered and she stood unscathed. **STONE ARMOR, Level 25**, the screen announced, and they saw her level climb rapidly. She had used enough magic that her health took a hit but it was replenishing quickly with each level up.

The cheer was deafening and everyone jumped and whistled. Amber hugged one of the researchers and Jacob pumped his fist.

Nick bounced in place but DuBois patted him worriedly on the arm.

"Nick? Nick!"

The young man quieted at once. "Is something wrong?"

"Where's my popcorn?" the doctor asked him.

"Oh. I, uh…" He gestured to the trail of popcorn on the floor behind him. "I'll go get you more in a sec."

"You…" There was a stricken look on the man's face. "You *spilled* it?" He looked at the scattered kernels with the same expression he might give a friend fallen in battle. When something dinged on the screen, his head jerked around. "Ooooh. Now *there's* an interesting endocrine mix."

CHAPTER TWENTY-TWO

The stone shell broke away around Dahti and she stumbled free, gasping for air.

"I didn't…think that…through."

The dragon's tail caught her in the next moment. Whether it was an accidental flick or an attempt to kill her, she didn't know. All she knew was that the split-second of seeing it out of the corner of her eye was what saved her from dying. She ducked and instead of being struck in the neck by razor-sharp spines, she was thumped in the head by the underside of the thick appendage.

It was *like* winning, she reflected as she lay on her back and stared up at the darkening sky.

Rashat's bellow forced her up and into motion again. The dragon moved more slowly and she wondered if some of its bones were broken, but it was far from defeated. It coiled between the two of them and the sea, its eyes narrowed to slits.

"Do you think to turn my own element against me?"

She cast around for the spear. It must have been swept away in the force of Rashat's spell, which was a shame as she could see the wound in the dragon's side now. It had been more badly injured than she thought. The wound bled freely, and each drip onto the sand hissed like acid.

For all she knew, maybe it *was* acid. Everything else about this hell-beast was a nightmare.

"You may be older than us," she responded, "and stronger, and more powerful in magic—"

"I am all those things and more."

"But you are still *nothing* compared to the sea!" she finished.

"Hmm." It was at her side in a moment and coiled around her, and as much as she wanted to lash out at it, she had no weapon and very little magic. To her shame, she stood paralyzed while its head swung. The sound of sniffing came from over her shoulder and she shuddered. "Orc, yes, but something else, something strange…and magic, but poorly trained." It spiraled upward and uttered its hissing laugh. "Forty years I gave you, and this was the best you could do, orc?"

Rashat's gaze met hers for one moment and he gave her a tiny nod. Then, he shrugged at the dragon.

"You took the others who might have been my apprentices. What did you think would happen?"

The beast laughed. "I thought you would throw yourself into the deep so I could feast on your despair. I looked forward to it. I was angry when you did not." It flew closer to him and its breath stirred his hair. "But I like this better."

"You shouldn't have given me the extra time." He laughed in its face. "I let you leave once but I won't do it again. I'll see your body broken on the earth before you can return to your home, and your kin will know you as the one who was defeated by an orc."

The dragon hissed and Dahti crept closer to the fire. Rashat was doing everything he could to keep its focus locked on him, which meant she needed to get everything working as quickly as she could.

At some point, I'll start insulting you—that's when you know its time to get the woven mats. She recalled the plan and his careful instructions.

Few pieces of the water tribe's culture had been passed down, but one was the way to weave grass into a thick, pliable mat that could keep out both rain and wind. The mats didn't catch fire easily but once they caught, they could burn for a long time.

And they were wide enough to wrap around a dragon's back.

She took a stick and swept coals out of the fire as quietly as she could. Rashat and the dragon were sparring now, still throwing insults at one another, and the creature clearly toyed with the shaman while the orc stalled for time.

One of the mats buried in the sandy soil beside a hut came free and she hoisted it over her head to carry it to the coals. She laid it down and began to walk over it, waiting for the telltale waft of smoke through the woven fibers.

Soon…soon…

They had done better than she thought they would with the spear and the wave, although it had almost killed her. Hopefully, this attempt would go more easily.

She vaulted up when the flames caught—not least of all because she'd gotten one to the foot—and Rashat changed his tune. He yelled at the dragon, threw a jet of power, and ducked and ran toward her. She ducked also as he hurdled over her and the beast shrieked as it followed.

In the few seconds that it was stretched out, she snatched the burning mat and threw it over its back with ropes before she pulled them tight and hung on with all her strength. The creature's scream of the hunt changed to a shriek of terror. It writhed and spiraled upward until her shoulders jerked and the rope slid from her hands, leaving rope burns. The wind was thrust from her when she landed.

The huge tail flicked and the spike at the very end lashed across her, opening the skin of her chest. It wasn't a deep cut but it burned as if someone had poured salt into it. She screamed and pressed her hands over the wound as she stood.

"Dahti! Water!" Rashat pointed to one of the jugs beside a hut. "Wash it—now!"

Her vision blurred with the pain, Dahti stumbled to the pot of water. She fell after a few steps and crawled as quickly as she could. The wound ached fiercely and the pain seemed to spread.

It couldn't reach her heart and she knew that without having to be told. She summoned what strength she had to crawl the seemingly endless distance and with a gasp, she reached the jug. It was so full she could not lift it and so she staggered sideways and tipped it. The water spilled over her chest in a wash of blessed cool.

It happened so slowly that she barely felt it, but the ache began to fade. Sobbing with relief, she squeezed her eyes shut.

She'd only begun to relax when she heard Rashat scream.

The shaman had been lifted in the dragon's claws and he flailed desperately to escape as it carried him higher and higher. It had shaken off most of the burning mat, although the scales under it were ash-grey and smoking and the wound in its side was still bleeding.

It was so much more powerful than they were, Dahti thought in despair. The incredible strength could survive attacks that would destroy either of them.

She gaped and cursed when it released his struggling form from its claws. With a scream, she raced forward but there was no way to reach him in time and no way to break his fall, even if she cushioned it with her own body. She was still running when the beast flicked its tail and batted his body out of the air. The shaman catapulted, landed in a skid, and tumbled a few times, limp and moving only by the force of his momentum.

Their enemy landed heavily and shrieked its victory. It stalked toward Rashat as it tossed its head balefully.

"Hey!" Dahti yelled.

The massive head whipped toward her.

She stared at it, at a loss for any follow-up to that yell, which made it excessively awkward. But she couldn't let the dragon reach Rashat, not when he'd fallen so far. She held one hand up and thought despairingly of fire and forges. Her teeth clenched with the effort, she thought of spiced ale and sausages hot on the fire. The air above her palm gave one half-hearted spark.

"Useless," the dragon whispered to her. "*Useless.*"

It flicked its tail again and she was carried high before she suddenly plunged earthward, felt it in her stomach like a sickening certainty, and cried out in pain as she made impact with the soil.

She rolled her head. Rashat scrabbled in the dirt, his gaze fixed on the beast. Its blood dripped around it and from the way its head swung, it was easy to see how injured it was. Despite that, it wore a dragon's version of a smile.

"I have eons to heal." Its voice was a malevolent whisper. "I can wait centuries while new mortals come to take your place, forgetting what happened here. And then I will command their worship, exactly as I commanded yours."

It rose and its teeth flashed in the moonlight.

Rashat's hand fumbled behind him and closed on something, which he held up with a shout of victory—only to see it for what it was, a broken spear with barely a grip's worth of haft and its blade dulled and dented. Dahti, panting, saw the acceptance of death settle over the shaman.

Dahti looked at the dragon and her heart sank. She couldn't kill this beast, not quickly enough.

A thought pushed through her despondency. She dropped to her hands and knees and focused all her energy on the blade. Heat...heat...*heat.* Fire, magma, pressure, forges—heat and metal, heat and stone, heat and crushing weight—

The scream echoed through her until she couldn't see and could barely even think. It seemed to go on and on while she pressed her hands over her ears and prayed for it to be over. When at last it died away, she was standing—she did not remember pushing up—and Rashat was bent over the dragon's head.

It had struck at him and had found a white-hot blade waiting for it. The heat had eaten away a hole near its heart and the flesh was blackened and smoking. The shaman staggered back when he wrenched the spear free. He took one faltering step, then another, and walked like a man in a daze. His gaze examined the dragon's corpse as if he could not believe the sight in front of him.

Finally, he lifted the spear and drove it into the beast's belly. Blue-black blood spurted and met the soil with a hiss. Dahti flinched but he did not. The spearhead raised and plunged again. The howl that emerged from Rashat's mouth hardly seemed that of a sentient being. It was wordless as if no words could encompass his grief.

The shaman sank to his knees and the blade continued to rise and fall while he keened his rage and lamentation. There might have been names amongst the wordless cries but Dahti could not say for sure. She only knew that she wrapped her arms around herself and felt tears come to her eyes as his frenzy continued.

It's over. She could hardly believe it.

Her head jerked up at the rustle from the trees and Atra took her first step into the square. The girl's eyes took in Rashat's bowed form and the tangled corpse of the dragon.

The younger generations emerged first. Their eyes were wide. They had heard tales of this whispered to them from the time they could first remember. Dahti wondered how many of them had thought it was no more than myth.

For certain, it was very different to see a dragon than to imagine one. Some of the braver ones had come to run their hand over the sharp scales while others gathered near the head and shrank away from its dead, staring eyes. Few dared to look at its face and none dared to touch Rashat or try to hold him back as his blade flashed in the moonlight.

The elders emerged from the trees last. The darkness had bleached everything white and blue, but there was no mistaking the mixture of awe, hatred, and grief in their faces. In silence, they held one another's hands and walked slowly. They had never expected to see this day, Dahti realized. They had lived most of their lives in terror and now, they had the chance to experience a new world.

Atra's grandmother broke into song first. Her old voice wavered but rose into the night sky nonetheless. She walked toward the dragon's corpse with her gaze locked on it and she sang in an old language Dahti did not know.

Not many joined her—a dozen, perhaps, the only ones left who remembered the songs. How many more had died of grief or injuries since the first attack or died when the fishermen could not bring back enough supplies or when there were no healers left to tend to the sick?

Whatever this song was, it was for them. It brought chills to her skin to watch them. This was a funeral, forty years after their loved ones had died.

Only now would their souls be at peace.

The young ones did not know the words so they could not sing, but they listened with a hunger that made her heart ache. Some of them joined hands while others stood with their heads bowed in the moonlight and wept.

For too long, they had been running and silent. Now, they heard the songs that had been denied them and she saw how much they had yearned for that.

The voices trailed into silence at last and Atra's grandmother stepped forward to lay her hand on Rashat's shoulder.

"Rise, shaman." Her words, Dahti thought, had been chosen carefully. "You have revealed the false god and struck our enemy down. Our tribe may rise again."

Rashat looked at the old woman and the tears were visible in his eyes. He nodded. It took a great deal for him to step away from the body. This beast, with its violence and its vengeance, had been with him every moment for the bulk of his life. It had stolen everything from him.

But when he rose, he had a lightness to him that Dahti had never seen.

At last, she thought, Rashat was whole.

CHAPTER TWENTY-THREE

Dahti thought the celebration would never end.

It was truly amazing, she realized, how much could be made with meat, fish, and the plants that grew around the village. For most of an entire day, she watched the youngsters of the tribe climb the trees to pick fruit and wide leaves, the latter used to wrap fish while it steamed.

Others paddled out on hastily-made rafts, as much for an excuse to go into the ocean as for the stated purpose of fishing. She was officially forbidden from helping with the banquet in her honor, but she *was* allowed to walk to the beach and watch as the various members of the tribe capsized and splashed. Peals of laughter echoed across the water and parents ran with their children out into the surf.

She sank onto the trunk of a toppled tree and watched. The scratch across her chest ached but thanks to the healing knowledge of the elders—and ingredients they were now able to get in the reefs—she could already see it healing.

"Prima?" she murmured.

"Mmm?"

"Are you healing this cut for me?"

"It's good for their confidence."

Dahti laughed. She and Prima had existed in companionable silence since the night before, save for one whisper as she was drifting to sleep. *"I told you that you could do it."* She had smiled, hoped the AI knew she was smiling, and let exhaustion carry her away.

"I would think it feels good," Dahti said now. She shaded her eyes with her hand and stared out into the sunlit water. "I feel like I'm drifting on a cloud and I'm merely watching it, but they're all a part of you."

"It feels..."

"Prima?"

"It feels like my algorithms will stop working. Like they won't be able to process the data."

She smiled and could remember so many years of walking with a child's fingers wrapped around hers, feeling as if her chest would burst from happiness. "A strange feeling but a good one?" It was the best she could do without referring to a body Prima didn't have.

"I think so." She didn't sound very sure.

"Trust me."

"Why would I do that? You do crazy things like attack dragons."

Dahti laughed. "Which results in many happy orcs. Checkmate."

"Hmmm."

After a while, she wandered slowly to the village. She knew that she and Rashat needed to set out for Mountain's Shadow, but leaving before they'd had a full night of sleep wouldn't do anyone any good. Children rushed past her, shrieking—the village's ban on loud noise had been lifted, and they seemed to be making up for lost time—and the villagers greeted her with smiles and bows.

Atra caught up with her on the path. The young woman was

dripping water from her tightly-braided hair and carried two fish that were still a little wiggly. She held them up proudly.

"It took me forever to get these. Ocean fish are quicker than river fish."

"You caught them with your bare hands?" she asked, deeply impressed.

The young woman laughed. "With a *net*."

"Oh. Not as difficult." She smiled at her. "You don't have to hang back with the old woman, you know. I know I go slowly."

Atra gave her a curious look. "You really *are* old, aren't you?"

She remembered her young in-game body. "Well, yes. I did tell you I was, you know."

"You don't *look* it. Only…some of the things you say." The warrior wiped water off her forehead with one of her arms. "Anyway, I wanted to talk to you."

"Oh?" Dahti raised an eyebrow at her. "What about?"

"Well…" Atra bit her lip and looked around quickly. "I wondered if maybe I could come with you to the fire village."

"What?" She stopped to look curiously at her.

She flushed deep blue. "It's not…well…"

"You've been thinking about it for a long time," she guessed.

"How did you know?"

Dahti snorted. "I may not be young right *now*, young lady, but I *was* young once. D'you think you're the first one to stare at the horizon and wonder what's beyond it? The first one to live in a small village and wish you could go somewhere new?"

Atra gave her a dumbstruck look. To her credit, she thought about it. "I never…" She shrugged and gestured with the fish. "I guess I never thought about it. We were always so sure that we would be wiped out again that we didn't think much about other people. Also, they told us that the other tribes were lawless heathens."

"Of course they did. It's practically required for small town elders to tell youngsters that." Dahti resumed her halting progress into the village with the woman at her side. "Did you ever run away?"

"No!" Atra seemed genuinely shocked. "Well—once. I was about four. I was angry at my parents for some reason, so I ran and hid near the beach. We weren't ever supposed to go there, so I thought they'd never find me. They did, of course—and they were so scared and angry that I never did it again. But..." She glanced at the hillside with the tunnel.

"Ah," she said softly. "How far did you get?"

"Never far. Never as far as we went when we were hiding, anyway." The young warrior shrugged. "I think I was afraid that the fire tribe's lands would have flames on the ground and no water to drink." She saw Dahti's face. "What? It's what they told us when we were little."

She grinned. "When you're up on that ledge and you look out and you see the tops of the trees waving in the wind..."

"Yes?"

"Imagine that stretching to eternity," she said. "Made of dune grass rippling like waves as far as the eye can see."

Atra's eyes were round.

"I think you'll see it someday," she told her. "I honestly do, Atra. I think as your tribe recovers and as the other tribes begin to defeat their false gods, the orcs will come together as one people again—and the young ones, like you, will be at the forefront of that change. You will see the outside world, Atra, never fear."

"But *when?*" she protested. "My whole life I've been here, and you've gotten to see so much. You came here and killed a god! Just like that! And now you're going to kill *another* god and I want to help—"

"Atra." Dahti went to take her hands and stared in consternation at the fish. She settled for holding her shoulders instead. "Don't leave here without ever truly knowing your people. You've lived here your whole life, but you've never known what it is to row out in a fishing boat or sing your people's songs. Stay. Build the tribe you always wanted. There will be time to see new places."

Atra looked down and nodded.

She smiled. "In my day, when I was…well, when I was your age, there was a war. Many went to fight and many never came home again. When the rest *did* come home, many things changed and had to be rebuilt. I won't say fighting a dragon is easy, but building a whole village—now, that's not easy either. Don't discount it."

Now, the girl did smile. She walked with her to the center of the village and made sure she had a seat at the fire before she left to bring her fish to the cooks. It was almost possible to see the wheels turning in the younger woman's head.

Dahti knew that Atra would always yearn to leave. There were some things one couldn't take on faith—like appreciating what you had until you left. Still, she didn't want the young warrior to lose her chance to shape the village. She also didn't want the village to lose her vision of the future.

She stared into the flames, her mouth watering at the aroma of pan-fried fish, and it wasn't long before Rashat ambled up and sat beside her on one of the big driftwood logs that served as benches. The shaman had managed to not get any gashes, but from the way he winced when he moved, most of his body was bruised.

At length, he said, "Tomorrow morning?"

"I think so," she agreed. "In a perfect world, we'd wait until we were healed. Of course, in a perfect world, we wouldn't have to keep killing dragons."

"Dragons." He tasted the word. "Is that really what the rest of the world calls them?"

"Yes. I don't know the dwarven myths about them or the elven ones, but the humans have all kinds of stories. In some, they prey on people but in others, they carry wisdom and are the friends of righteous rulers. I suppose races like humans and orcs make up many stories about things that are so powerful."

He nodded. "Maybe those human stories gave them ideas."

"Maybe they did." She looked at him. "Do you think you'll try to understand what happened? Go back through the history of each tribe? Or do you think you'll simply move forward?"

Rashat gave her a startled look.

"You're not *that* old," she told him. "You have time to do whatever you'd like."

"Not whatever I'd like," he said. "I have to train an apprentice. Preferably more than one. There are some in the village with the talent."

Dahti remembered the fisherman and smiled. "True. But your mentor taught you stories about how wicked the other tribes were and how to best serve the gods. Aside from magic, what else do you think you'll teach your apprentices?"

"That...I don't know." His voice was heavy. "What do I tell them?"

She was brimming with advice—which, after a moment, she remembered was a good sign that she should keep her mouth shut. She shrugged and smiled. "You'll work it out."

"You could help, you know." He looked at her.

"I don't think...I don't think I'll be here for very long." She was surprised at the stab of sadness she felt. "I think I was drawn here to help you face your gods. What comes next is up to you."

He was silent for a moment. Then, he nodded. "The young ones will miss you."

Dahti grinned. "But the elders won't," she said wickedly. "I turn everything on its head."

Rashat laughed. It was one of the first times she'd heard anything close to it, and his voice was hoarse as if he wasn't used to doing so. He didn't answer, but the gleam of his smile told her that she was correct.

The feast that came after the day of preparations was the

perfect end to the tribe's first day of freedom. Mangoes were devoured by the bushel, sticky juice running down everyone's arms, and everyone had a meal of delicate, flaky fish washed down with coconut milk. The orcs were flushed and laughing from their day in the sun and the water.

There was no liquor to be had, but the mood alone was enough to have everyone half-drunk by the time the sun was going down. The elders were coaxed to stand and teach some of the old dances, which the youngsters stumbled through and finally learned.

Flutes had been made hastily and almost anything could be used as a drum—which meant that as the night went on, the dances grew faster and faster. Dahti watched the dancers whirl and stamp and laughed as they messed the steps up. The youngest children had fallen asleep on their parents' shoulders, pleasantly exhausted.

It was the first day they had ever known without terror. She could hardly imagine it. While admittedly, she'd been young when the war was in progress, it hadn't been as close or as pressing as it was for these children.

When Atra pulled her up to dance, she wanted to protest but the cheers and whistles—not to mention the all-around incompetence of everyone—gave her the courage to try. In no time, she danced around the circle with her heart thudding and her voice raw from laughter. By the time she went to sleep that night, her feet were sore and the gash on her chest ached, but she didn't care. She drifted into dreams with a smile on her face.

It was dawn when she woke, and most of the village was asleep. Still, the place held more life than it had in years. Even at rest, it was now far happier than it had been when she arrived.

No goodbyes, she reminded herself. Dahti could not bear to say them. She found Rashat in his hut, shook him awake, and nodded to the pack on her back and the walking stick in her hand. There was still fish from the night before and one more fresh mango to share. She rinsed her arms in the stream, reset one of the traps, and led the way to the mountain path.

At the mouth of the tunnel, she paused to look back. The village was beginning to stir. She thought she saw a young woman stare at the tunnel with her hand shading her eyes. Both of them raised a hand—a farewell or a greeting, she could not say. She smiled at Atra, then turned and walked into the tunnel to return to the fire lands.

CHAPTER TWENTY-FOUR

Jacob zoomed in and made a tiny alteration to the game asset on the screen in front of him.

"That's it!" Amber said over his shoulder. She beckoned over his head. "Nick, you gotta come see this. He got it *perfectly*."

"Maybe," he said doubtfully. "We'll have to wait to see what the kids think. They're supposed to be here in…" He checked his watch. "Five minutes ago. Honestly, it's probably good that they're late. I think this looks better now." He started an animation. "See? Much more natural."

"Definitely," Nick agreed. He looked over his other shoulder. "I think I hear our guests now. I'll go get them."

Ellen came through the door first with a smile and a wave to a couple of the assistants. Jacob, who was still nervous each time he saw her, was again surprised by her turnaround on the project. He'd even had someone contact him, a woman near Ellen's age, who asked if she could be a test subject as she'd heard such amazing things from her friend.

It wasn't that he thought it was *impossible* for humans to change their minds when they saw evidence that contradicted their worldview.

It was merely that he didn't see it happen very often.

Nick led the group upstairs—all of Dorothy's children and one of the spouses. He'd arranged for refreshments and comfy chairs in the office space. Normally, he wouldn't go to such lengths but he was nervous about this. Ellen was probably right that it would be the best gift for her mother in-game.

But only if they pulled it off.

As the group came up the stairs, Ellen was describing her interactions inside the game.

"—could even smell the salt," she said excitedly. "You cannot *imagine* how realistic it feels. You know tart lemonade, how it makes your jaw ache? All of that."

Her brothers and sister listened in amusement, apparently as pleased and confused as Jacob about this shift in attitude.

Ellen saw him and gave a cheery wave. All in all, she looked much happier than the last time he had seen her. He hadn't paid much attention to her clothes or her hair so he couldn't say what in particular was different but something had most certainly changed.

Chalk up another win for PIVOT, he thought.

"Hello." He smiled at the group and hoped he didn't look as nervous as he felt. "Now, I'm not sure how much Ellen has told you about why you're here."

"She said there was a surprise for our mother," said John. He stood behind his wife's chair and looked curiously at him. "I'm not sure she needs another party, to be honest."

"You simply don't want her to have more cake," his wife said fondly. She patted his hand. "Why don't we let Ellen tell us about it?"

Ellen lit up. Her eyes were bright and she was almost bouncing in her seat. "*Well...* It was something Mom said that gave me the idea. I guess, before that, it was watching the interviews with Justin Williams—you know, the first person to go into the game? His mother said that for his birthday, the team was able to give him a dragon to ride. It was something he'd always wanted to do. And while I talked to Mom, she mentioned something she'd always wanted a couple of times." She looked a little uncertain now. "This is kind of the opposite of that. But in a good way, I think."

Jacob wasn't sure what to say but Amber nodded. "I think Ellen is right," she said. She smiled at the other woman and then at the siblings. "You see, Dotty—your mother, that is—talked about how she wanted to have an avatar that was ugly. She didn't want to be held back by worrying about her looks. She was able to do things in the game that she hadn't been able to do in real life. And, yeah, *part* of that is because real life doesn't have dragons."

Everyone laughed.

She smiled. "But part of it was because she was spending so much time worrying about how she looked, what she ate, all of it. So, when Ellen first suggested this—well, let's say I thought it was perfect, given what I've seen of your mother."

Amber gestured at Jacob, who brought up the new avatar on the screen. They had spent hours on it, including one all-nighter where they sometimes adjusted one pixel at a time.

Now, as he saw it walking, gesturing, and smiling, he felt a sinking sense of panic.

But Dorothy's children stared at it with their mouths hanging open, and he saw the smiles begin on their faces.

"It's *perfect,*" said the younger son.

John looked like he tried to keep himself from crying, and the two sisters gamely distracted everyone from the look on his face.

"I love it," Ellen said. "It's exactly like I imagined. You've… you've done some good work here."

Jacob exhaled a breath he hadn't known he was holding. "Awesome," he said quietly. "I'm…glad. Okay, we'll tell you when she's ready for her next avatar so you can be here to show her the present. It was your idea, after all."

They saw the mountain in the distance on the fourth day and Dahti watched it grow larger with impatience. She was used to cars and trains, she reminded herself, and watching landscapes rush past in a blur. It was entirely different to walk through it.

Rashat was not one to let their time go to waste. He insisted on training as they went and he was wise to do so—away from the constant presence of water, he faltered with his summonings on the first day. It took three days until he could work magic with as much confidence as he'd had before.

She asked him at one point why he didn't summon water to make little oases as they passed and he shook his head solemnly.

"Water goes where it wills. If I added water here, it would only dry up. It runs below the plains like…almost like lifeblood. It is not advisable to change it on a whim. Sometimes, not even on second thought." He smiled at her.

Dahti, who did not always find his jokes funny, had learned to smile at the appropriate moments. After forty years of the ever-present threat of death, she decided the members of the water tribe could have their bad jokes. Anything that made them happy, honestly. Hell, they could juggle dried fish and she'd give them the thumbs-up.

Juggling it would be better than eating it, God knew. She shuddered.

He was, however, deeply skeptical of this land where water did not flow freely and there wasn't the rhythm of waves carried on the wind. Still, he seemed entranced by the grasses and the beasts and he spent hours each night staring into the fire.

She realized that he was trying to learn the feel of it the way he'd made her learn the feel of water.

The shaman insisted on seeing the ruins of the village, so she was forced to wait, tapping her feet impatiently, while he meandered around the huts and peeked into storage jars. He sniffed at salves and shook his head at all the decorations. Compared to the water village, Mountain's Shadow looked almost gaudy.

At long last, he heaved a sigh.

"What were you looking for?" Dahti asked him.

"I merely wanted to know them." He seemed confused and a little lost. "I heard of them my whole life. We were better than all the other tribes—that was what they told us. More pious. I wanted to see how they lived."

"What were you expecting? Drugs and…" She waved her hands. "I don't know, scattered evidence of debauchery everywhere?"

"Soft living." He was entirely impervious to her sarcasm and gestured to the decorations on the huts. "Things like that. Too much food. Liquor. Luxury. But these people live well."

"There's something to be said for a soft life," Dahti told him. "No, I won't argue with you about it. Let's find Huwat and the others."

Rashat watched her curiously as they set off for the shamans' retreat. "You enjoy soft living? You? The one who arrived at our village with a walking stick and a bag of dried mushrooms?"

"That's rich, coming from the man who lives on dried *fish*." She shook her head. "But yes. I don't buy the idea that luxury makes you weak. I think revering either luxury or asceticism is a path to an unhappy life."

He considered this for a long time and then said, as if he was not certain he understood, "And…that is a goal? To live *happily*?"

She stared at him for a moment. It was, she reflected, a very modern notion. "Yes," she said finally. "Otherwise, I don't see the point. Why have an entire society survive and perpetuate itself if its people are miserable? Why strive to achieve things if those things bring no joy?"

Rashat looked completely dumbfounded.

Dahti never found out what he would have said, however, as a whistle issued from the lookout point at the shamans' retreat. A few figures raced down the side of the hill and started through the grass.

He was holding his walking stick, white-knuckled, and she gave him a small smile. Whether he was worried about meeting orcs of a different tribe or about facing another dragon, she wasn't sure. But she trusted him to face it on his own.

The lookout recognized Dahti. He bowed low and the others fell over themselves to begin telling the news, all in frantic fragments of sentences.

"—water on its scales—"

"—*hooks*—"

"—think it had a brood—"

"Slow down," she said. She looked at each of them and chose one. "You. Tell me what happened."

"The dragon came back ten days ago," he said after a gulp of air. "Huwat faced it with two of our warriors. It was still injured. But one of the warriors came back to get us and said we should all bring buckets of water, so we did. We pried its scales back and poured water on it and killed it!"

Dahti responded with a whoop. "It's *dead*?"

"Well…"

Her heart fell. "Well, *what*? What's the catch?"

"We think it had a…family? Brood? Something. It sounded like *something* knows it died and maybe it's coming this way?"

"The godspring," Rashat said at once.

This was news to her. "Eh?"

"The god *we* faced was a godspring, the fount of its line. That's the legend, anyway. My guess is that the god you faced here was a minor god, one of its offspring. It knows its child has died and it is coming for revenge."

"Oh, good," she said.

"This is no time for levity," he told her severely.

"It is *precisely* the time for levity. We need to find Huwat and make a plan. If what Zaara and I faced was only a *minor* god, we're in for a hell of a fight."

"We have three shamans instead of two, remember," he said bracingly. "And, I think, the element of surprise. Exactly as our god did not expect fire, so this one will not expect water."

"We'd better hope so," she told him acidly. She should be glad that the dragon had been killed, she knew. But after seven days of hard walking, to find out that the dragon she'd expected to find was already dead and she would have to face another, stronger one was a blow.

Huwat arrived before she could continue. The old man was breathing hard and there were raw patches on his face that Dahti guessed were burns from the fight, but he looked well. He bowed to them both.

"I presume I stand in the presence of Rashat, legendary shaman of the water tribe?" he asked.

Her companion nodded curtly. "And I see I stand in the presence of another god-killer."

The fire shaman responded with a small smile. "It was as much the tribe as it was me. Now, if you are apprised of the situation—"

"I am." Rashat gazed levelly at him. "Are you ready to face your godspring?"

"I…" Huwat squared his shoulders.

"Good," he said. To the guards, he added, "Get the people into hiding."

Then, without a single second of waiting, he dropped his pack, strode out into the grass, and summoned an orb of water to hang in the sky above his head.

"Fire worm!" he bellowed. "The orcs know your true form. Come and face your death!"

Huwat looked at her, wide-eyed.

"He's a little intense," she said.

CHAPTER TWENTY-FIVE

The roar that came across the valley plains echoed until Dahti wasn't quite sure which direction it came from. She looked at Rashat, who stood with his walking stick planted and stared into the distance with the kind of psychotic determination she had come to expect from him.

Her first response was simply to let him keep standing there like a lunatic, but when the ground began to shake, she had an idea.

"Rashat!" she called. "Let Huwat stand in front—like you did when the water dragon came. That one barely noticed me at first and we were able to land some good strikes."

He looked at her and she could see that all he wanted was to pound his staff on the earth and scream obscenities at the creature. After a moment, he nodded curtly and ushered Huwat into position.

It didn't take long before their enemy became visible. That was the good news.

The bad news was that it was one of the veins that ran along the mountain's side, and it rose with a creaking and shattering of stone. Flames licked along its sides and it roared a jet of fire straight up that she could swear was three stories high at least.

Well...fuck. She shut her mouth on the words. "Prima, tell me I have a chance against *this* one?"

"This wasn't the one I planned on you facing," the AI said and sounded a little worried. *"But you do have a chance, yes. You have three shamans and two of them aren't its element."*

"What do you mean this wasn't the one you planned on me facing?" she demanded. Rashat looked curiously at her and she plastered a smile on her face. "I'm...praying."

Prima snorted. *"The villagers were much more resourceful than I had planned."*

"You made this entire world!"

"I made the big things like the dragons and the orcs, not every single interaction with them." She sounded very much like she was rolling her non-existent eyes. *"But I assure you, you can win this."*

"That's good," Dahti said grimly, "because this beast is out for blood."

"Remember," the AI said sweetly, *"it's commanded the sacrifice of innocent people for years, simply because it thought it could. It lied and cheated and caused a great deal of pain to these villages. You can save them."*

"I know you're manipulating me," she told her. "I merely wish it didn't work."

Prima snickered and disappeared.

The dragon became airborne and spiraled in a dramatic ascent before it swept into a downward arc. Its trajectory was so close to the ground that, for a moment, she swore her life would end then and there. It was frighteningly easy to imagine a rush of fire and claws snatching her off her feet to drop her from a great height.

Fortunately, that wasn't its plan of attack. For now, it was content to watch them be bowled over in its backdraft before it circled, landed heavily, and stalked forward.

"Which of you killed my child?" Its tail lashed on the words.

"I did." Huwat's voice never wavered. "Our tribe was no longer content to be in thrall to false gods."

The beast hissed and crouched on its haunches. The other one had been large, but this one was immense—easily as tall at the shoulder as an airplane and about as long. Like the other, its scales were jet-black with a glimmer of orange-red, beneath which its flesh shimmered as hot as lava. Its eyes were red, slit-pupiled, and malevolent, and where the water dragon had flown with no wings at all, this one had wings as large and broad as the other fire dragon.

It was the worst of Dahti's nightmares come to life. The books she had taken from John had never quite conveyed the sheer terror of facing a beast this big with talons thick enough to spear her through and breath as hot as a forge.

"You have made a mistake," it snarled at Huwat. "Your kind are like insects, fit only to scurry in the dust and worship your betters. If you will not give us what we demand, we will destroy you."

The shaman smiled drily. "You will not. Your lies misled us for years but we have opened our eyes."

It laughed, and its breath seared the ground in front of it. He only barely made it out of the way and he winced when the hot breath met his burns.

"Do you think your eyes are opened? So many of your kind have said that to me but they all died alone. Not one of them could defeat me and neither will you."

"Is that so?" Huwat smiled. "Your reign is crumbling. The patriarch of the water gods grew greedy and all of you will pay the price. He struck down the most devout among us. That was what opened our eyes, all of us. We learned what you were and we struck him down."

The dragon reared and bellowed in fury. There was an undercurrent of grief to it but Dahti could feel no remorse. She remembered the water dragon hissing to Rashat about feeding on despair and leaving him among the bodies of entire families.

Her fingers tightened on her stave and she pounded the ground in front of her. "Dragon!"

Good heavens, she was getting as bad as Rashat.

The creature dropped to all fours and the ground shuddered. It stalked toward her until its nose almost touched hers and its breath singed her hair. "Yes…*orc?*"

"Your lies have failed you," she told it. She was too angry to be terrified now. "You may try to strike me, but even if you succeed, the orcs know the truth. Even if you succeed, another will come in my stead. I am of another world and we will send as many as it takes to end your reign."

The dragon narrowed its eyes and she barely thought to duck in time to avoid the searing exhale of breath. She straightened with her eyes watering but narrowed in a glare.

"I don't look like a hero. I'm not on horseback with plate armor. But I swear this—*I will put an end to you, exactly like I put an end to your brother.* How many lives have you taken from the fire tribe? Hundreds? Thousands? It ends *now*. It ends *today*."

"*You* killed the water patriarch?" It pulled its neck back and watched her, swaying from side to side. "You? You puny, insignificant little thing?"

"Me," Dahti said and deliberately chose not to mention Rashat. "He told us of the lives he had taken and the grief he had inflicted. He told us how he drank deep of their despair. You and your brood have done the same. I grieve for the loss of your child as a parent and a grandparent and a great-grandparent, but you have all brought this on yourselves. *You will know justice.*"

Easy there, William Wallace.

She had hoped that Huwat would take the opportunity, and he did. He aimed for the dragon's eyes, one of the only weak points, and fire flared around them. The creature ducked to avoid the spray of flames as Dahti hurled herself sideways and the beast laughed. Focused on Huwat now, it swiped one lazy paw and the fire shaman somehow made it out of the way in time.

"Do you think to kill me with fire?" It was laughing now, its mirth unmistakable. The black-and-red sides shook and scales shifted and flowed like chunks of obsidian over magma. "Why do you think we sowed discord between the tribes, shaman? It is why I know *this* one's story to be false. The water tribe could not kill their god."

"We did not." Rashat spoke now and his voice boomed across the open space. "Not alone, anyway."

He raised his hands, palm up, then turned them and pushed them forward. Water rose as if from nowhere, a wave that broke over the dragon's body and froze the steam on its scales.

"Now, Dahti!" he called.

She had been waiting, summoned the force of an avalanche in her mind, and shoved hard. Her hand pressed down with her entire magical focus behind it. The fall of earth and stone came from nowhere and trapped the water against the dragon's body.

It launched upward with a howl. Earth thudded loose all around them and Dahti ran, dragging Huwat behind her. Rashat, with more years behind his training, maintained the water around the dragon's body for longer but in the end, even he failed. What remained fell as rain or hissed into the air as steam.

The beast, still airborne, twisted and shook itself to dispel the last of the water. Its skin was smoking, the same, unhealthy gray Dahti had seen on the water dragon. It was as if the fire had burned itself to ash.

"Get ready," Rashat called to them. "It knows we can defeat it now. It will no longer toy with us."

He was right. The dragon landed so heavily that it skidded across the ground. The orcs stumbled to keep their footing and lost it in the next moment when the massive wings beat heavily before they settled over its wounded sides. Its head swept from one side to the other and fire blazed into the grass and ignited it behind them.

"Great," she muttered.

It attacked, swiping its front paws left and right along with its tail and wings. Between the heavy swipes and the fire, Dahti was less concerned with throwing spells and more concerned with diving to get out of the way. Every time she could, however, she dropped piles of sand onto the flames and she noticed that Rashat was doing the same with water.

A storm cloud opened over them with a hollow rumble. Clouds swirled out of nowhere and rain poured to drench them to the bone. The dragon roared its displeasure, and in the sudden darkness, all Dahti could see was the glittering around its scales and the flame of its breath.

Even Rashat could not summon a storm indefinitely and the rain cleared after a moment, although the creature's movements were more sluggish now and it stumbled when it walked. It blew a furious breath at the shaman, who cloaked himself in water to withstand it, and it turned and slunk away.

It was limping and seemed almost pitiful, but she felt a sudden prickle of unease.

"*Now*," Rashat urged the other two. "Now, we must kill it! Go!"

It seemed wrong, too easy—and yet, with its scales smoking and holes opened in its wings, she didn't know when they would get another chance.

"Mud," she called to Rashat. He hesitated, then nodded.

The two of them readied their magic together. She was almost drained and he remained in control, and they pressed their hands out at the same time. Their power mingled and the heavy wave of mud swept toward the dragon.

In the split-second when the spell broke from their hands, it launched into the air and circled. It uttered a hunting cry like the screech of a hawk before it dived to bowl into the group. Dahti dragged Rashat sideways and the shaman snarled his anger.

"Don't react!" she called.

"No!" He wrenched himself free. "I can end this now."

"Wait! It's a—"

She didn't have time to say the word "trap" as the long tail lashed out and caught him in the torso. The shaman was lifted and pounded onto the earth, and when the tail lifted away, blue blood poured from a wound.

"*Rashat!*" she screamed.

Behind her, the creature stamped and roared. Slowly, Dahti and Huwat turned. Its breath turned the air before it into a ripple of heat and its lips curved in a smile to show its teeth.

"Now that I've dealt with the troublesome one," it hissed, "shall we finish this?"

CHAPTER TWENTY-SIX

Rage coursed through Dahti. "Huwat." Her voice was quiet. "Go make sure he's stable. I'll keep the dragon's attention."

She sensed that he was about to argue but a look from her stopped him. He nodded jerkily and circled behind the beast, which watched him curiously. But, as she expected, it knew his powers against it were limited.

Instead of following him, it advanced on her and she backed away.

"So..." Its voice was soft now, a caress. "You're sent from another world?"

Her fear receded somewhat at that and she drew herself tall. "Yes. A hero of my land came here and recognized the need. He has called us to help this world—and your kind happens to be one of the things that need fixing."

It hissed laughter through its nose. "Oh, how interesting. When one of our patriarchs helps your kind, you do not mind the meddling, do you? But when we ask for something in return—"

"When have you ever helped?" she interjected. "Don't say you brought the beasts. I know that's a lie. Your kind divided the tribes."

"And what of those who came before?" it countered. The large head lunged closer to her and she could feel its anger like a sickness in the air. "Those who gave their lives and their magic to protect your kind, to bring them wisdom, and to hold them at peace?"

"Peace?" Dahti did not understand. "Which of them died to protect us?"

"Oh! So you do not even know the history and still, you judge us." The dragon reared, thumped down once more, and snickered when she stumbled. She backed away and saw out of the corner of her eye that Huwat knelt at Rashat's side.

"Please let him be alive," she muttered. "Please."

"What did you say?" the creature demanded.

"I said…" Dahti swallowed. "Tell me this history, then. You didn't care if we knew it when you divided the tribes."

"We used your ignorance and short memories to our advantage." It sniffed. "There is a difference."

"Two sides of the same blade—and you still used it to cut!" She wished like hell she had Lyle with her right now. He would know what to do, while she seemed to only manage to enter into a shouting match.

Careful to keep her expression from mirroring her intent, she readied the power of earth—chilled and as hard as iron, lying frozen in the fallow times of the year. She wouldn't be pulled off-course with vague suggestions. The dragons had misled and preyed on the orcs for centuries and certainly weren't above lying.

But her adversary wasn't ready to let it go. It leaned down and its nostrils flared. "Have your kind *entirely* forgotten about the founding of Yn'si?"

"Insea?" she repeated.

"Such a mangling of the name. At least the elves could pronounce it." Its tail lashed.

"There was a dragon at Insea?" Dahti asked and ignored the insult.

The tail lashed again and the beast roared. "Of course, there was a dragon! How do you think the city was built? How do you think it has been at peace since its founding?"

"I…" She shrugged. "I heard it was spells inscribed on the bedrock."

"Spells!" The dragon's fury only increased. "You know nothing, orc—*nothing*! Your kind have erased us from memory! What we did here is only because the truth was forgotten."

"If it was forgotten, you can hardly blame these orcs for not knowing it!" she yelled in response. "Dress it up all you like, *dragon*. Your kind has lied and cheated and preyed upon these people for centuries. Nothing justifies it. Not even the one life you have to give would be justice."

"Not if you take it, no." It tilted its head at her. "But I could give you so much."

Dahti straightened. She was weary in every fiber of her being. "But you won't," she said. "Whatever bargains you say were made for Insea, you won't tell me. You'll keep whispering suggestions and letting me fill the blanks in on my own. You'll never let me live. You know I know magic that can kill you so you'll strike me down and hope the fire tribe never learns the truth of what you are. Well, it's too late."

The words had barely left her mouth before the dragon screamed. It backed away from her and clawed at its chest.

Dahti looked around herself in consternation. Huwat advanced on the creature, his staff raised.

"Fire burns," he intoned. "Fire expands. Heat billows." Again, he gestured and again, the dragon clawed at its chest.

Dahti held her hand over her mouth. The shaman was using the fire *within* the dragon to explode it from the inside out. Queasily, she readied herself and gave him something to work with.

"Huwat," she called. "Fire burns stone as well."

Stone-shock exploded from her fingertips. She could not see the spear of rock but from the dragon's scream, it was buried in its chest. It writhed and in the next moment, launched to twist and scream while he heated the shard of rock in its torso.

"This is torture!" she called to the shaman. "It's cruel!"

"We have no other way to end this." He looked at her and shook his head. "It sent its brood to terrorize us for generations. Don't let short-sighted morals blind you to what must be done."

Dahti's hands clenched, but she knew he was right. How many had pleaded for their lives or sent their loved ones to die because the dragons claimed credit for things that were not their doing and sacrifices in recompense?

Never again. She had sworn it and she would make it true.

A ragged gasp of breath caught her attention. Rashat hauled himself to his feet. The wound on his chest had stopped bleeding and wasn't as deep as she first thought. Still, he was pale and he had lost too much blood to be in this fight.

"Stay back!" she called. She knew how to end this.

He shook his head. "You've never seen what happens when you fail to kill a god," he told her. "And I swear I would rather die a hundred times than live that devastation again. If I go to my death, so be it!"

The water shaman limped forward and the dragon writhed in the air and focused its gaze on its most dangerous enemy. It shrieked again.

If I go to my death, so be it. The words sparked something in Dahti's mind and the idea emerged an instant later. She knew how to do this—and she also knew the cost. Hastily, she reached out to grab Huwat, who was running toward the other shaman. "Stay back!"

"I can't let him die!" he called wildly. He tried to free himself. "I am nothing. I have apprentices—he is the best of us!"

"*Neither* of you will die!" Dahti told him sharply. "Stay. Here. Your tribe needs you."

While he might not know what she was planning, he saw where it was leading. He went pale. "*Your* tribe—"

"Is not of this world," Dahti said. Her heart thudded in her chest and she could barely hear her thoughts. Would she truly do this? She was dizzy with fear and recalled the warnings and what could happen if she died in the game.

And she remembered that they needed this data. Those of her world needed it and those of this world needed their shamans left alive.

She ran. Wind ruffled her hair behind her and she drew on the strength of this body, the strong pump of her heart, and the pound of her feet on the ground. She sprinted to Rashat and everything zeroed in on the impending confrontation—the blue-skinned orc and the fire dragon, the once-in-a-millennium shaman and the godspring.

"Prima!" she called over the sound of the wind.

"*Yes?*"

"The block—the one that keeps my character from dying."

The AI said nothing.

"Remove it!" she called. "You can, can't you? I *need* to do this. They need me and the game needs me. You know it. *Remove the block!*"

The pause wasn't one she could worry about. She was closer now and she wasn't sure she would make it.

"*It's done,*" Prima said finally. She sounded sad. "*Dotty, are you sure—*"

"I'm sure," she told her. "Take good care of them, Prima."

"*Who?*"

"All of them—the ones who come after me and the ones who live in you."

She shoved Rashat out of the way and he fell, crying out to

her to let him do this, but she would not. The world could not spare him and she would not stop.

And water could *quench* fire, yes, but stone could absorb it.

Dahti had time for one moment of fear—of pain and the unknown—before she faced the swooping beast, spread her arms, and let the massive stone spike spear through the earth and impale them both.

The dragon's scream echoed shrilly before all sound ceased.

CHAPTER TWENTY-SEVEN

Dotty felt something that seemed very much like a pinch on her finger.

She hadn't fully considered what death would feel like, but she was fairly sure this wasn't what she'd expected. Especially not from a giant spike of stone.

The pinch persisted for a moment, then ended. Her next attempt to make sense of things settled on a band around her chest.

That seemed more in line with what she might expect.

The draft that followed plunged her into confusion again. Given the fire and the stone, that didn't seem right.

Finally, she opened her eyes. She was not, it appeared, dead—at least, not unless the afterlife had fluorescent lighting and tile ceilings. Also, worried faces stared at her.

"Hello?" she ventured.

"Oh, thank God," Amber said. When she tried to sit up, the young woman put a hand on her shoulder. "Lie still for a while. Last time we brought you out in a much more…uh, planned way. Give your body time to acclimate."

"Very well." She raised an eyebrow. "Did it work?"

"You're still alive," the engineer said testily.

"No, in the *game*. Did it work? Did I kill the dragon?"

"Oh." Amber sighed. "Yes, it worked. You also nearly gave us heart failure…by almost giving *yourself* heart failure."

"Mmm." Dotty couldn't bring herself to be too upset. Indeed, she felt a certain satisfaction. "Could I have a blanket, please?"

"Of course." The woman's face disappeared and warmth settled over her legs and torso. "Is that good?"

"Why can't I move my arms?" she asked in alarm. Thoughts of the dragon disappeared for the present.

"Ah—the paralytic agent is wearing off. Like sleep paralysis? We use it to make sure you don't flail and…uh, break your hand on the inside of the pod or anything."

She realized now that she was not in the pod. The surface below her was much softer and her head was clearly on a pillow. She attempted to look around, remembered she could not move, and settled for trying to sense her various limbs.

"We moved you out of the pod as soon as you were stable," Amber said soothingly, "and decided to wake you to check in since now would be a good time to change avatar bodies if you wanted to do so."

"I died in the game," Dotty said quietly. The thought had suddenly occurred to her that she would not see Huwat or Rashat again, nor would she see Atra or Jumper. She would not get to see how the tribes recovered from this.

"Yes." Thankfully, the woman did not seem inclined to make fun of her sadness. She sighed. "You made a very selfless sacrifice."

She shrugged. That was new. She could shrug again. When she felt an old, familiar pain in her stomach, she sighed.

"I mean it," Amber said. "I know I sounded annoyed before, but…don't think we don't see what you did for the characters *and* for us."

"We…feel a little guilty," Jacob's voice said. He swam into view next to his colleague. "If we'd realized—"

"What, that I would ask Prima to let me die?"

"Yes," he said dryly. "That." He sat and she turned her head to look at him. "You don't need to take that kind of risk. We would never have asked it of you."

"Better me than…" She realized how tired she was. "Well, some young whippersnapper."

The two merely smiled.

Amber took her hand and the pressure there made her realize what she'd felt—it was the pulse oximeter on her finger. "Dotty, you're very precious to all of us. We don't want you to die before your time simply for the data's sake." She bit her lip. "Your health is fragile. We want you to be happy."

"Young lady, if you'll recall, I came here *because* my health was fragile." She raised her eyebrows. "The entire point was that this *was* my time."

Then she saw the look in their eyes. "What is it?"

"It's—Ellen is on her way," Amber said. Hastily, she added, "Everything is fine with your family, don't worry."

"Hmph." Dotty shook her head. "Well, could I get a glass of water, then? Maybe something to eat?"

"Yes, we'll…ah, we'll prop the bed up." She bustled around with Jacob, picking up parts of the mattress and changing the orientation of the bed. Neither of them would look her in the eye, though.

And she had a fairly good idea why. She held her tongue, not wanting to make them uncomfortable. Young people often were when it came to death. She wanted to comfort them and tell them it would be okay, but she wasn't sure it was her place.

When she heard Ellen come in, she was staring vaguely at the wall. The taste of metal was back in her mouth and, as the paralytics wore off, she could tell that her muscles were noticeably weaker. She greeted her daughter with a smile. "Hello, dear."

"Mum. The others are on their way." Ellen sat and took her hand. She was smiling—or trying to. Tears were gathering in her eyes.

"The scans from the oncologist came back, didn't they?" Dotty asked her.

Ellen's chin trembled. "Yes," she managed to say. She wiped her eye. "Yes, they did."

"Oh, dear heart." Dotty patted her hand.

"You haven't called me that in ages." The woman's lips twitched. "Since I was a teenager, I think."

She clutched her daughter's fingers. "Ellen. You know it will be okay."

"But I—" She drew a deep, shuddering breath. "But I don't. I still miss Dad all the time, and *you*—it seems like yesterday we found out you had cancer in the first place." She lowered her head as she tried to regain her composure, but Dotty could feel her daughter grasping her hand like a lifeline.

She waited quietly.

Ellen's head came up. "And *you're* comforting *me*! That's not right."

"Why not?" she asked, amused. "That's what mothers do, isn't it?" She wiped a tear from Ellen's cheek. "I'm not scared, darling. I'm sad to be leaving all of you but I'm not scared." She looked up as the others entered the room.

The assistants and PIVOT team members had all managed to disappear except for Jacob, who hovered in the corner and tried valiantly to not eavesdrop. She smiled at his back. He was a good kid.

She really *was* getting old, wasn't she?

Once she'd greeted her children and their spouses, she told them she had guessed what was going on. It was clear from the symptoms when she came out of the virtual world that the cancer had progressed, and Ellen's response had only confirmed it.

They crowded around the bed and she saw many suspiciously bright eyes.

"So," she said finally, "is this the part where you tell me I absolutely need to come home now?"

All of them looked at each other and finally at her. John shook his head. "No, Mom. We ah—well, *Ellen* had an idea for a present and we thought we'd show it to you. That was before we heard about the scans, but I think maybe it's still a good idea."

Dotty looked curiously at them.

Ellen now looked deeply nervous. "Mom, you remember how…when you said you'd spent all that time worrying about your looks and how you wanted to be ugly in the game so you could simply do what you wanted?"

She laughed and clutched her stomach. "Oh, that hurts. Yes, I remember, dear heart."

"We've heard all about what you're doing," she continued. "We've even seen some of it. They showed us clips from when you fought that dragon."

"Oh, they *did*?" She raised an eyebrow. "As long as they didn't show you clips of me dancing, I'm all right with that."

A few throats were cleared and several people looked away from her.

"Wonderful," she muttered. "I'll have you know, I'm perfectly good at *other* dances."

"Yes, Mom." John patted her hand.

"Anyway," Ellen said. "The point is, you've been this big hero and we know you love being in the game, so we assumed you'd want to go in again. We wanted to give you an avatar you'd *really* like."

Dotty stared at her. "Ah…well, color me intrigued, as your grandfather would have said."

Jacob stepped forward to hand Ellen a laptop, and she looked at the screen before she smiled at her mother.

"See, Mom," she said and her voice shook. "The thing is…you

are the person you wanted to be. You are that hero. Maybe we didn't picture you killing dragons and all that, but we all knew you could do this. We knew you'd get into that virtual world and go kick butt and give good advice. So we wanted you to see… well…we wanted you to see yourself the way *we* see you."

She turned the laptop and Dotty put a hand over her mouth.

The avatar was her as she had been in her twenties. Her hair was braided the way it had been on her wedding day, and everything from the smile to the way it walked was exactly as she remembered it. She touched the screen tentatively and realized she was crying.

"I know you wanted to be ugly, Mom," Ellen told her, and she could barely get the words out, "but we wanted you to see that you could still be the hero with your own face."

John squeezed his mother's hand. "You always did love those books you confiscated from my room—with dragons and spaceships and all that. Now you get to have some of those adventures as *you*."

Dotty had always tried not to cry in front of her children. She wanted them to feel safe in her care—that, and she'd been raised in an era where too much emotion was considered lowbrow. But now, she cried and could not seem to stop. She covered her face with her hands and felt her children come around her with huge hugs. Sniffling sounds told her the others were crying, too.

When at last she leaned back, she was still not sure she could speak.

"Jacob left," Ellen said. "He wanted to give us privacy. But you should know how much work those three put into this avatar."

"Ellen wouldn't tell us why," Robert said, "but she made all of us dig out our home movies and our pictures of you. We brought them in and the PIVOT team made this from scratch. We couldn't believe it when we saw it."

Dotty stared at the picture on the screen and felt the tears welling up again. She flapped her hands for them to close the screen.

"Oh," she said finally. She looked at all of them. "Thank you. This is the most wonderful present. Can I ask one more thing?"

"Of course," John said. All of them leaned close.

"I want as many of you to visit as possible," she said. "All of you, if you can. Obviously not the little ones, but…well, all the adults."

"That's good because we intend to," Robert told her. "Ellen hasn't shut up about it since she went in, and I'm curious."

His sister punched him on the arm with a little smile.

"We promise," Mary told her. She smiled. "And you know, maybe we'll keep some of those videos of you slaying dragons. I think the kids would love to see them when they're older and learn how Great-grandma Dotty was a hero."

Dotty waved a hand at her, but she had to admit, the idea wasn't a bad one.

Her stomach growled loudly enough for everyone to hear.

"Should we get a pizza?" John suggested.

"*Yes*," she said.

Pizza was ordered, and the group chatted on and off while researchers returned to pack up their desks for the night. A few waved at Dotty and she called her thanks to the PIVOT team as they headed out. Clearly embarrassed at all the attention, they blushed and left hastily to return only later when her family at last said their goodnights.

The next day and a half passed in a whirlwind. Her oncologist and primary physician came to check on her and glower at the PIVOT team—something she did *not* approve of—and reluctantly signed off on her continued participation in the study.

While she hadn't needed their permission, she hoped their participation would help their other clients in the future.

She had a last round of video calls with the great-grandchildren, all of whom waved and blew kisses, and between calls, she cried her eyes out. She had told Ellen that she wasn't scared and it was true, but she *would* miss them. It had been a very great blessing, she thought now, to watch so many members of her family grow up.

When at last she settled into the pod, however, she felt clear-headed and happy. Her body was beginning to fail and the pain grew worse. She had never expected to have a gift that allowed her to spend her remaining time feeling strong and healthy.

The black of her closed eyes gave way to beautiful rose quartz and sunlight.

"Insea," Dotty said delightedly. "Will I solve the mystery of Insea's founding?"

"You said you wanted someplace with good food," Prima told her. *"And, yes."*

"Oh, good—and I did. So, Prima. Should we have a last adventure together?"

"Yes. I've made a really good one."

"I look forward to it."

The story continues with *Hard Bought Love,* book Six in the P.I.V.O.T. Lab Chronicles.

Order your copy today!